AF492891

THE BLACK

PETER WANJOHI

A NOVEL

THE BLACK

This is the first edition of the Original title:
The Black, published in 2024.
eBook and Paperback editions
Text in this book is set in EB Garamond 11.5, Roboto Mono 30, and Oswald 11.5
Cover/Interior/Editing by Arikana Publishing.
Nairobi, Kenya.

ISBN 978-9914-37-151-2

Copyright ©Peter Wanjohi, 2024
A copy is also available from the Kenya National Library.

Email: Admin@Arikanabook.com
Phone: (+254) 0113864310
www.arikanabook.com

Instagram: @officialArikana
Facebook: @Arikanabook

All rights Reserved. No part of this book publication may be reproduced, stored in a retrieval system or transmitted in any way by any means (electronic, mechanical, photocopy, recording or otherwise) without the prior permission of the copyright owner except as provided by copyright law. No part of this book may be used or reproduced in any manner for the purpose of training artificial intelligence technologies or systems.

Contents

CHAPTER 01

6000 BC. Venus.

The night sky was glowing red. Suddenly, a loud explosion marked the atmosphere. There at the sky's edge, metal debris rained down on the planet. *'A spacecraft? Possibly one of the escapees.'*

Below the chaotic sky, atop the pinnacle of the planet's highest skyscraper, *Flocky* stood watching. His rank was adorned; the leader of the men of the black race. He gave a glance to the neon display upon his right-hand wrist, then back to the sky. Not even the crashing of the waters in the reservoir beside the building could steal his attention. Without a flinch in his eye, he watched as the frantic race to escape the planet ensued, and ship after another blew up on reaching the glowing red blanket.

As quick as the events unfolded, a young man came from behind him, bearing news. "Flocky the *edifice* is ready." Flocky remained still, eyes fixed up and answered, "Okay, launch it now–before it's too late."

"We are waiting for you. It cannot launch without you."

"No, I am going to stay here on the planet with my people."

"But, the plan...You are our leader! We cannot allow you to perish like those commoners!"

Flocky became uneasy. He then turned to the man and said,

"That's my choice to make then, isn't it? And I choose to die today. I was warned this day would come..." He looked below from the magnificent skyscraper.

"All this wealth, and for what? The greed ends today. Our people will be much better starting somewhere else. This lust has made us so blind– I will die here. As long as I stand, none of the odd council will have a chance to plunder what I have built! We must pay for my sin, in full!" Then the man responded, "No. Come, save yourself! Look. Your vindication; the edifice–that is your legacy now! You funded our only salvation!"

Before Flocky could respond, the sky rumbled! The two stood in line, staring at the sky, terrified. "That's the sulphuric rain coming." Flocky said, turning back to the young man, "Go! Teach our ways to the new world. To a new generation..." Before his words were done, there came a tumultuous quake, parting the ground beneath the skyscraper! A gaping crack then swallowed the very place beneath Flocky's feet, and he fell.

Upon the peak of the monument bearing the heights of his ambition, Flocky lay unconscious. The skyscraper, once believed to be the strongest building on the planet, had a long stretching crack running from the bottom to the top. It was sure, another quake would shatter the building into rubble.

The man dashed off to where Flocky lay, trying to wake him up. He shook his body to revive him, frantically calling his name. Several attempts in, Flocky woke.

"Quickly, get up. We need to flee!"

"It's too late now." Flocky groaned, frail in the man's arms, who strived to get him back on his feet. All the time, Flocky watched his right wrist.

"There is still some time left," The man insisted.

Flocky looked back at the man, his face with little regret to it.

"It is done. We will meet in the next life."

He reached for his wrist, pressing a button. Then, a loud siren filled the already panic-choked air. It was enough to bring the planet to a halt, and everyone looked at the skyscraper where the two were.

It was then that the reservoir beside the skyscraper slowly opened its mammoth gates. The reveal of a magnificent craft from within its bellies brought awe to all who witnessed it. A feat of godly stature! With ease, it raised above the skyline, thrusters revving to full power, plunging past the red glowing blanket. All that looked up, realised what had transpired, leading in a chorus shout:

"To Victory!"

Flocky mastered the last of his strength, screaming at the top of his lungs:

"Long live our race."

A glint of a tear fell from the height of the skyscraper, and as the spaceship sped off into the great pitch black, vanishing to the billions of stars, the entire planet exploded.

Nothing remained but floating dust.

Current time in Kenya.

The late-night air was disrupted by a loud whirring noise. A helicopter hovered above the Menegai crater, spotting a secret station East of it. Upon landing, two white men in full black stepped out, briefcases clasped at hand and walked towards the edge of the helipad. There, a scrawny fellow in a white dust coat stood expecting them. After an awkward handshake, he led the men away to what seemed like an obvious rock formation from the outside. Then, upon nearing, there appeared a large hidden cave opening. "The thing that we found has left us with more questions than answers."

The cave was lit up within, men busy walking up and down. They moved briskly past them, as if invincible to the pandemonium on the floor, heading straight to the furthest corner of the cave. They boarded a metallic capsule, a lift, lowering them into the earth's crust at the command of Mr. *Dust coat*.

"I want you to carefully observe the temperature as we go deeper." The men followed the pointing of his frail finger to a thermometer on the lift's wall, displaying a reversing count of degrees, as their depth increased.

"This defies every logical principle that we know about the earth's core!" *Dust coat*, a scientist added. The Lift stopped, as there was no more ground to descend, opening to a mechanised floor within a dredged cavity beneath the facility.

One of the men finally spoke, "It's...cold."

"Exactly!"

"...And what are your findings on this phenomenon?"

Dust coat replied with a foolish smirk, "Something down here is absorbing all that energy! But, we don't know what it is." He proceeded to produce an old compass from his dust coat, "Here, come close..." The two men stood around the scientist, curious.

"Is it broken?" The man asked further.

"That's what we thought at first, but this was recalibrated this morning..."

"Then, why is it doing this?"

The scientist replied, "In Theory, this can only occur in a high energy zone, like a black hole. The magnetic field here is *super* unstable!" The man pressed, "So there is a high energy source here?"

"Yes! But this is the farthest we can go..."

"Why so?"

"We tried to drill through. We ended up breaking a dozen drills. This surface–the element it's made of, it's harder than metal!"

"Have you tried bombing it?"

"No. That remains the last result. A bomb, *if* capable of breaking this surface, will cause massive damage to the Menengai crater."

One of the men laid his hand on the scientist's shoulder, squeezing in, "What are you waiting for? Do it." The scientist's countenance folded in fear, "But–what about the crat..."

"You will get me what's beneath this surface, even if the crater's got to go!" Cornered, the scientist's brow began to sweat, "Wouldn't that cause too much of a scene? I mean, it is a much-regarded scenery by the public. And besides, how can we evacuate this entire place on time?"

"I want it done with immediate effect..." The man squeezed the scientist's shoulder harder.

"...And make it look like a natural occurrence. I don't care if you take a few casualties, Just Get It Done!"

Grave silence followed this exchange. Before the scientist could answer, they heard a noise.

Sounded like a creature.

Immediately, the men reached inside their black suits, eyes scanning the entire floor. Then, right beside the turn, next to one of the pillars holding the cavity above, they saw a man deep asleep, snoring.

One of the men went forward, and using his leg hit the fellow with haughtiness. He woke up, confused. Slowly removing his hand from his chest, the man asked, "Who are you?"

"I–I am just a worker here." He answered, showing his work tag.

"What are you doing here?"

"I am sorry. I was working and then fell asleep."

The scientist jumped between them, "He is just one of our *diggers*... they work day and night. You see, they need the money to sustain their families." After seemingly de-escalating the situation, the scientist turned quickly to the worker. "Go. Make sure to have adequate sleep." The worker nodded, running off to the lift, beating up buttons on it frantically, so it went up.

"And what if he heard our conversation?" The two men convened, their faces straight.

"He was asleep. He couldn't have heard a thing," the scientist defended. *Words to a stone*.

"We don't work that way." The man asking all the questions, asserted his position, dictating to the second, "Make sure he doesn't meet any-body." He did not linger, following to see to it.

Otis was lazing in bed while reeling on some socialite on his instagram. Sleep was fleeting, and yes, he fancied her. You could tell by how many messages he had sent into her inbox of late. *A distraction for the time being.*

It was his second month after Uni–a victim of the evergrowing unemployment bubble in the country. His days were largely spent running errands for his folks, and sending out applications every other day. His uncle had promised to make something out of his papers' worth, but such was the situation. Then, his phone popped! A red emoji! He sat up quickly. 'She liked one!'

He bit his lip itching to answer. Right then, a knock came up. He sat still, waiting. It resounded, this time louder. It sounded like it came from across the hall.

Otis spunk off his bed, leaving his phone on the covers. He followed the succession of knocks on the main door, peeping through the dark to see who it was. He immediately opened the door, meeting a middle-aged man catching his breath, beads of sweat on his forehead. In his hand, a work tag–*excavator engineer*.

"Dad, what's wrong?"

"Nothing Otis. I'm just home early. Where is your mother?"

"She is sleeping."

"Okay, lock up the door," Otis's father responded, as he walked past him towards the master bedroom.

As Otis looked on, something didn't add up. Usually, if the work didn't dry out his father, hunger would finish him. Only, he did not go looking to fix a plate.

"Aren't you hungry?"

His father looked back at him. "Son, if I was hungry, I could have asked about it. I need you to shut that door now. And do not let anyone in, do you understand me?" Otis heard the slight rattle in his father's voice. *'Something's up.'*

He looked out to the calm and chill street. The coast was clear. He closed the door, latched in place and double-checked.

Back at the site, the scientist's dust coat flapped in the wind, as he stood next to one of the white men; the *senior-ranked* man. From a distance, the other white man walked towards them. "He is gone. I cannot find him."

"I don't want to hear it. I want the man dead!" The senior-ranked man barked, turning to the scientist. "If the information of our *plan* is leaked, this establishment, all the research money, all these workers — All that will go down the drain! We do not want that now, do we?"

The scientist answered, "Don't worry about him. We have a record of all our workers, their shifts, where they live and who they live with. It will be taken care of."

Morning found Otis asleep in his bed. Suddenly, he heard a loud knock on his bedroom door, then. "Otis!" His mother called. He sluggishly got out of bed.

"A minute Mom..."

"I don't have a minute!" She was getting impatient.

"Do you know what time it is?" Her anger resounded after the door opened.

"But mom, I was..."

"You should have started on your chores by now. I am going to be late, and have you seen your father?" She was disgruntled, as Otis followed her half-awake.

"He came in last night. I thought he was with you."

"What do you mean? Otis, don't be lying to me!"

His mom stopped in her tracks of grumbling, and before Otis could explain, another knock came at their main door. He watched her face go from boiling anger to full-on confusion. She turned to the door, quietly leading the way once more. A bold figure shadowed their entrance as she swung the door open. Otis stretched and yawned, quickly catching a glimpse of those at the door through their open sheer curtains. *Another suit.*

"Are you *Irene*, Jeremiah's wife?"

"Yes, why?" She answered, her face showing every ounce of emotion within.

"There has been an accident at the site. There has been a caving in. Sorry to break this news to you, but your husband was one of the casualties..."

"But—he was here. He came home last night. I spoke to him! Mom..." A whirlwind of questions stirred in Otis's mind.

"The body is still buried underneath it, and a recovery of bodies has begun. Again, so sorry for the loss."

Irene, Otis's mother, held on to her robe. Otis fell back, stunned at the news. Anything else that followed out of the man's mouth felt like muffled babbling. All holding *nothingness*.

"It is ok. You can go." Irene hurried the man out. As soon as he walked away, Otis's mother gently shut the door behind her.

She lowered her head, moving to clasp Otis as if he were the one in need of comforting.

It bothered Otis that her cheeks did not run a tear!

CHAPTER 02

Noon.

Otis sat on a curb beside the road moving up their street, alone, watching cars. He was sure–more than sure that he had encountered his father the previous night. He remembered the smell of his father's working shirt, wafting past him. The cracking in his voice resounded. Even his uneasy walk to the master bedroom. Otis felt it. Like it was happening all over again. What he did not understand was why his mother seemed a little too well-seated with the news. Was she hiding something? *'Very strange.'*

For some time, his friends had had conspiracy theories about his father's job.

He was so engrossed in thought, that he didn't notice the young kinky-haired woman sitting next to him. *Ivy* was one of his friends from childhood. There remained a warmth to their friendship, even after all the years of schooling and distance. She sat quietly for a while, watching how Otis put his fingers through his tough hair and immediately she knew. "Are things Okay, Otis?"

"Could be worse, I guess...you?"

"Well, now that you asked, I've spent the last 5 minutes checking out every car model driving by. It's tough to decide on the car I'd like to drive." She turned to face him.

"Otis, you know I can tell there is something wrong. Everyone keen enough to look can see it."

"It's that obvious, huh?" Otis turned to Ivy.

"Remember when you lost your new pencil back when we were kids? Like, You got the tongue-lashing of a lifetime from your dad, for a pencil! The funny thing is, you had actually offered that same pencil to me a day prior, and just didn't want to tell your dad. You're the most kind and *alright* guy I know."

A shy Otis chuckled, "Only you could call that–*alright*."

"And a little crazy. But not like crazy, crazy. Just a little weird. So, what's letting you down?" Ivy being there was yielding comfort for Otis. He sat up, eye to eye with Ivy.

"Yesterday my father arrived home late. He acted–strange. I think it's because of that site he works…"

"…I knew it! You see. I always told you there was something off about that place! But you just couldn't stomach my *'hocus-pocus'*." Ivy jumped, then fizzled down on noticing the look on Otis.

"I am sorry. Please continue."

Otis stood from the curb, "Ivy, a man came to our door this morning and told my mom that my dad is dead! I have no time for your nonsensical conspiracy theories. *Sheesh!*" He stomped his foot. Ivy then stood up slowly, bearing an awful calmness. "I am really sorry Otis. I didn't know…"

"Some friend you are!" Otis huffed, walking away. Ivy ran after him. "Otis–I am so sorry. I didn't mean to be disrespectful. Stop!"

Ivy reached for Otis's arm, as Otis held back tears. "We have always trusted each other, Otis. I am sorry. Hey, I mean it..." Otis turned to Ivy's empathetic face. "...Perhaps you should stop for a moment and just listen first. It's not always about being right all the time, Ivy."

Ivy retracted her hand. "And how is your mother doing? Anything I can do to help?"

Otis replayed that moment at the door. "She acts like—It's like he was never there. It hurts because I saw him come home. I did. But there she sat holding me like...like I am the only one who had lost him or something."

Ivy became curious, "Perhaps your father knew it all along. Perhaps she was hiding..."

"Stop it, Ivy!" Otis stormed off, fuming.

Right at the edge of the road, a rowdy voice came, "Hey guys!" Ernest burst upon the two in his usual charisma, offering Otis a fist bump, "*Nakucheki na mrembo*, bro!"

"Now's not the time." Ernest's energy died off immediately.

As Otis walked further along, Ernest turned to an upset Ivy, "*Kwani*, what happened?"

"Well, Otis lost his father," She sighed. "But Something's off about him..."

"Oh man, that's tough. Maybe it's best to let him walk it off. He'll come around when he's ready," Ernest tried to calm Ivy.

"I sure hope so too. He always has."

Three canvas-mounted semi-trucks trailed the high and dusty road to the site's establishment. The Menengai outbacks had been bought out from the locals. It was said that big checks had gone around, not just to buy their silence but to also keep people from asking questions about the work there.

Otis hid on the Southern edge of the site. He watched every activity at the Site's entrance, as the trucks were being checked, noticing a breach in the fence. Ivy had successfully planted doubt, poking holes into his already budding questioning. He sneaked about the parched earth, behind the abundance of lush thickets, rolling right under the cut barbed mesh. He was curious. A dangerous kind of recklessness that wasn't the usual Otis. *What if he got caught?*

For a moment, the swelling uncertainty blinded him to act. Act foolishly–or perhaps, bravely. Otis crouched, watching the expansive field, leading to a large tent ahead of the cave. It remained surprisingly unbusy. He ran up to the side of the tent, falling next to a set of crates behind it. He kept fixated at the entrance, seeing armed men escort one of the trucks, as it reversed towards the tent. He saw a 4 cubits box, like a coffin drawn from the tent. As it was, his curiosity pushed him to investigate further, risking blowing his cover. He crouched once more, sneaking past the crates, to have a closer look.

Before he could get there, a loud vibration rocked his pants. He stopped, baiting his breath. Then, he felt his pockets, intently pulling out his phone. 'Argh! Battery is dying.' He spiralled towards the tent's surface, lining himself thin on it, while putting away his phone. He bit his tongue, quietly proceeding with his pursuit. He pushed to a tiny space between the truck and the tent, hoping to catch the conspiracy for himself!

Then, at the entrance, an array of arsenal and explosive-ready C4 was on display. What Otis saw rocked him to his core. He was taken aback by all this. 'What are all the explosives for?' He hurried to pick up his phone so he could take *evidence*, but he was startled by gunfire.

He fell to the ground, lifting his eyes from the dust. There, right at the tent's opening, a man was on his knees, begging two of the armed men for his life, "I am sorry. I didn't intend to—It was my mistake. It won't happen again..."

"We will make sure there is a zero chance that mistake is repeated," said one of the gun-toting men, sneering at the man. Two shots were fired. The man dropped dead, eyes cold at Otis.

'Shriek!' Otis almost bit the ground.

"What was that?" The gunmen asked, looking around. "Go there and see!"

Otis's heart jumped to his throat, as a heavily built man in boots and gear marched towards where he was. *'Uh-oh!'*

In a moment, Otis rolled under the truck and kept silent. His life depended on it. It did. He saw the blood-stained boots beat the dust where he had lain. An AK gun's noose dangled down suddenly, flaunting its smoky pout of death right before his sweaty eyes.

"It was probably the wind on the tent!" The man spoke in a heavy baritone, turning back. "Let's clean it up. Throw it with the rest."

Otis's pupils widened. *'The Rest?'*

He gave a breath, releasing the tension he had lunged in. He had seen enough. He then sought to roll out from underneath the truck. On his last turn, another vibration shook his pants. Ignoring it, he rolled again, meeting a clean pair of boots firmly planted right before his forehead.

"Boy, you shouldn't have come looking for trouble here," a eerily familiar voice said. It was the last he heard before a cold metallic blow rang behind his head. He saw darkness!

The metallic ringing quickly returned, then vertigo with a heavy set dull ache at the back of the head. He felt the tips of his fingers, as a rush of cold moist air rushed to his lungs and he coughed. Consciousness. When Otis came to. He felt heavy like he was tied to a rock. Then, the cold floor turned liquid. 'Where are my shoes?'

"Back to the land of the living?" again, he knew that voice but not with the kind of peril it now attached itself to. A light poured out from above him. Tinnitus sounded in Otis's ear as he tried to shield his eyes, noticing the rugged mouldy rope tying his wrists together.

"You do not walk into my facility unannounced," From the dark, a man in black pulled out a chair barely showing his face. "Young man if it were up to me, you could be dead by now. But, you are lucky. Someone came pleading on your behalf. Now I consider myself a kind person. I have a good heart, you see. But, those men out there–they have ice in their veins. I convinced them to spare you. You are alive. I've kept my part. You better keep yours." He stood, veering off Otis's sight. Then, a woman was thrown into the light, whimpering over his face, "My son! Did they hurt you? Are you okay?"

"Mom...Mom, I am fine." Otis groaned.

"What were you thinking going there? You know better..."

"You two are no longer my problem," The man asserted in his bossy tone. "If you find it a habit to cross other people's fences where you are not supposed to, I will not stand in the way of anyone again, you hear me and hear me well boy. There will be casualties!" He wrapped up his coat, walking away into the pitch blackness.

Otis could not feel on his face. His mother spread her sweater's ends patting his swollen eyes, both bloodshot.

"What did they do to you?"

"Mom, Why did you lie?"

"Lie about what?" His mother paused, looking confused. "Otis, I have already lost your father. I cannot afford to lose you..."

"You–you did not cry for him. You did not even question it when the man said Dad was dead. I told you I had seen him. You didn't believe me!"

"Otis," She realised his rage. "I have shed enough tears already. They did not bring him back. You are all I have, and I will not allow you to..."

"...Turn out dead, like him?"

His mother's eyes became still like life left them for a second. Her hands retracted from Otis and onto her chest, her fingers carefully tugging on her necklace. Otis saw it–the *gift* from her husband from their anniversary three years prior.

In that silence, two men in police clothing walked in. One cut Otis's tethers, the other taking his mother away. "*Uko na bahati sana wewe kijana. Hawa sio kama afande wasamehe!*" He pressed Otis in the stomach, "Take your shoes and follow your mother. Quick!"

Otis sat quietly on a stool next to a wall charger. The room smelled of freshening lavender. It was warm and dimly lit. He took out his phone. 'The idiots must have bugged this.' The screen was cracked, and still black. He took out a white charger, waited a minute, and then it gave a beep. He sighed in relief. He felt the nape of his neck. The ache was dying a little, throbbing from time to time. Then, the phone started beeping again. He checked to see if the charger was in right, only to see a flood of missed calls aligning on the cracked screen. *'Mom...I don't have energy right now!'*

He put it to silence and turned the phone backside up. He looked across the room and smiled. He stood up, taking light steps and squeezed in right next to where Ivy snuggly fit. He laid on the covers, watching her breathing. 'Everything will be fine tomorrow.'

As soon as the day broke, Otis walked out with Ivy to the front of the house. "I need to get back home. Thank you for giving a lost boy some refuge," Otis said in what was more of a whisper. Ivy smiled briefly, as she turned the key on the door, careful not to wake her folks. They walked up the road, side by side, not exchanging a word.

"That was really stupid of you," Ivy's croaky voice came.

"But, I had to know..."

"You don't do that, and I don't care whether you are grieving your father or not, but that was very inconsiderate Otis. You could have been killed."

"I am alive, aren't I?" Otis brushed off Ivy.

"If half of what you told me last night is true, those people are more dangerous than I thought. You better watch yourself." Otis turned to Ivy for the first time since they had started waking, "You are concerned, huh?"

She composed herself, "Your mother Otis...she is the one you should think about. You've got to go and apologise. She needs to see you." Otis did not answer, lowering his head. "Thank you–for everything. Like, you have been too kind to my unkindness." She shook her head, then fit her skinny arms around Otis's back. He embraced her, and they parted.

On arriving at the front of their house, Otis found an eerie scene. The neighbours were standing at a distance, solemn. 'Mom!' He dashed off past the curb, meeting a broken door. Inside, the house was turned upside down, not a frame of glass left intact. Not a piece of furniture whole! Then, a trail of thick dark red markings on the runner led to the master. His heart sank, and his mind went blank.

"Mom! Mom!" He called out, panicking. Then he saw the necklace–the one his dad had gifted her from their anniversary. It lay there, right under him, broken in half. His knees were weak. He knelt to retrieve it, "Mother?"

He remained there on the floor, devastated.

CHAPTER 03

Underneath the cave. Deep beneath the surface, was a chasm. Dark, cold and quiet...

Suddenly from above it, a loud drill penetrated the ceiling. After a meter radius hole was drilled, torch lights poured down. Ropes followed, with men in anti-radioactivity suits descending onto the *virgin* place. Behold, the impenetrable surface hid under its guise a black... *thing*–like a large edifice!

One of the men signalled further descent, around this...*thing*. The men reached the cavity end around it, amazed at how well preserved it was. Investigating what they were looking at, Steve, who led a team of 5 men, watched the screen floating on his suit, "The radiation is much stronger here." He led the others towards where the energy seemed to emanate.

Above them, on the floor where the Cave's lift ended, two men monitored the operation on a large mainframe. Then, the dots on the screen began to blink.

"What could be the problem?" The one standing asked.

"It seems we're losing their signal," said the man seated operating the mainframe, punching up keys on the computer. "What? That cannot be..." The man leaned in, squinting his eyes.

"Steve is the best there is! Their tech is impeccable!"

"I don't think it is Steve's gear that is faulty. Whatever is down there is jamming the signal."

"Try again. I am not getting another team down there!"

"I am trying...*huh* If anything, the signal is perhaps only lost on our end. Steve will have to go on without our guide."

"Here, look!" Steve pointed his flashlight down a man-sized groove, underneath the *edifice*. The men followed in a broken chain. Then, a chirping sound was heard behind them. They all stopped, "Did you hear that?" They turned to see one of the team, precariously holding a cubic block.

"Kelvin, what's that?" Steve asked.

"Not sure. It fell off the wall. Looks like a...oh!" The cube blinked, and suddenly, a cracking sound of terror came up above and around them. "Put that down, right now!" Steve warned, as the rest waded away from where Kelvin stood.

"Alright, alright. Let me put it back..."

"Steve, look!" One of the men pointed to the screen. "The radiation—it has stabilised!"

Everyone was perturbed. He then moved to slowly take off one of his gloves. "Feels...feels normal," he said in amazement.

"Nobody take off your gear! We don't know what any of this is. We must proceed cautiously. Kelvin put that *cube* back! Everything must remain intact!"

As the men proceeded, Kelvin lagged seeking to undo this anomaly. The men came to the end of the groove, meeting a smooth hardy surface. "What do you think it is? An entrance of sorts?"

"Only one way to find out," Steve felt for controls on the surface.

"Something's down here..." One of the men bent, pointing at an ankle-high horizontal cut on it. Steve continued to map the surface, until, *'Voot!'* A stagnant beam shot from behind them, onto the walls of the groove.

Then, there came a loud vibration upon the surface. The men quickly stepped back. "Is this *thing* alive?" Steve pointed his flashlight towards the direction from which the laser came, blinding Kelvin, who dropped the cube. It blinked again, and the beam began to move towards the men! "You fool! You were supposed to put that back!" Steve shouted in a panic.

"I thought to see what else it could do..." Kelvin said ducking the beam, falling to the floor. 'That's oddly hot for a light beam.' Kelvin saw it etch the groove's wall above him, "Everybody down! It's a laser!" The men followed the warning and fell, letting the laser pass above them. Kelvin moved quickly to join the others, leaving the cube behind.

"This is a death trap!" Steve reckoned, focusing on the surface before them. "There's no other way but through–"

He was interrupted by screeching in his ear. He pressed his earpiece deeper, "Mission control! Mission control! Are you there?" He started to walk around, seeking a clear signal. Then a resurgent voice crackled, "...Steve? Can-you-u He-ar me-e?"

He signalled one of his men to keep decoding for a passage.

"I can hear you, Mission control! Talk to me."

"Steve, what's happening down there? What's disrupting the signal?" came a clearer voice.

"It's hard to describe the scene. We found a hollow cavity beneath the surface, a kind of alien edifice! It seems to hack our systems," Steve explained, looking back to where the cube fell. He walked towards it, "We've hit a kind of dead-end here...We cannot break through to enter it."

"It's coming back!" Kelvin warned Steve, who was engrossed in the details of the cube. The laser appeared again, right before them. Suddenly, the burning laser broke into three parallel beams!

Steve's eyes widened, "Men, we need to break through that surface right now if we want to live!"

"We might need more time to get past this!"

"Use the C4! Try everything you got, damn it!" The voice on the earpiece shouted.

"Here!" One of the men threw a pocket-sized pack. "Plant it on the wall!"

Steve rushed back, tailing him, 3 laser beams!

"Everybody, down!"

A thunderous blast shook the premise, the impact of it flattening everyone!

Steve woke to a loud ringing in his ears. Dust and shards everywhere. He felt his suit, then slowly rose to the call of Mission Control, "Steve! Is everyone okay?"

"Affirmative..."

"Steve!" Kelvin reached him from within the resting dust. He brought him in, only to see one of his men chopped up to three.

"Steve! Did we lose you again? Can you hear me?"

"No. I am here. We lost one."

"Oh–" the voice responded. Another insisted in his ear, "Listen, Steve. Focus on the task at hand. The edifice–Did it break?" Steve looked up to see the surface: "Barely scratched!"

"What is this thing made out of?" One of the men said, crawling up to it in frustration. A strong sense of desperation arose. Before the weight of inevitable death had settled, "The laser...it's returning!"

Steve's earpiece suddenly went silent. Kelvin watched his boss, like a pillar of salt, gazing at the air thinning between them and the incoming beam. Then, it multiplied to a mesh, covering the entirety of the groove, wall to wall! Kelvin's eyes ransacked the place, searching for something. Anything to hold on to. Then, "The cube! Steve! We've got to try it!" There was no response, only fear.

Kelvin ran forward thoughtlessly, as the men edged further back. 'I Hope you're right this time...' Steve watched, as did the others. Kelvin fell forward, grabbing hold of the cube. The heat of scorching lasers was apparent.

'Alright cube, do your thing!' He said to himself, lifting it. *Nothing!*

His heart started to rush. "Try putting it back!"

"Right!" Kelvin sighed, trying to find the space on the walls.

Steve looked back, seeing the man in charge of decoding for passage frantically trying to peer through the open slit below them.

"How close are you to figuring that out?"

"Not Very..." He said, almost out of breath. Steve stared back at Kelvin. 'You're our last hope, fool.' He marched forward, "Do all you can to break through!" Ahead, the laser beams burned brightly, more neatly together than before.

"Leave it! Come back!" Steve panicked, an arm's breadth away from

Kelvin.

"No, I almost have it!" Kelvin tried fitting the cube onto the punch hole on the wall. Steve saw the tight space, shrinking. "Maybe we'll find luck on the other side, come on Kelvin! Quit being so stubborn!"

Kelvin refused to answer him. Their suits started heating up, as the lasers burned closer. Quickly, Steve yanked him away and they fell. Kelvin rolled past Steve, looking up, "That's it!"

Before Steve could grab him again, Kelvin threw himself at the Laser's front, drawing out the cube, and then he fixed it back and immediately, the slit upon the surface stretched upwards, and a passage opened.

"Kelvin!" Steve hurried up to his feet, dashing towards the open passage, right behind his men. "Right behind you!" Kelvin shouted, the lasers racing up. Immediately the last man crossed the passage, it closed. The men each took off their helmets, gasping for air. Steve looked to Kelvin, and a grin was inevitable, "Saved us once again, Kelvin."

With the lasers no longer a problem, they were quickly made aware of the strange site they had been *swallowed* into. They waited amid a pathway, not sure whether to go left or right, "Now what?" One asked. Steve reset the screen on his hand, "Now, we finish what we came to do. Energy's coming from this way..." He led them to the left, warding the men to keep a distance. The longer they walked the pathway, the warmer it became. Then, before them, a mammoth opening to a large hall. At the centre of it sat a blue glowing cube. Steve turned to Kelvin, "I will handle this one."

"You don't have to tell me twice!" Kelvin nodded. The men stood away, eyes out in case it was a repeat of what they had seen, "Careful now!"

He proceeded to feel the cube, but his hand went right through it! "A Hologram?" A loud click stunned them. Before they could move, a stone rolled from atop the openings, trapping them in.

"That's not the control box!"

Then, the screen started beeping uncontrollably. Steve tried resetting it, "No. No. No. That's not right…"

"What's not right? Steve?"

"It says that all the radiation it sensed earlier is filling this hall!"

"All our helmets are outside…" A grievous look dawned on each of their faces. The hall turned grim. 'These radiations are off the charts…' Steve heard a ring. It tore through his head, growing by the second, bringing him to his knees, palms tight on his ears. Right then, the screen on his arm broke down. The teeth-gnashing ring cringed and prolonged, until–utter silence.

All the men were on the floor, fainted, some bleeding from their ears.

From the ground, a shadow rose. Steve's eyes were cold and empty. His poise was yet to stabilise. Then, a primal rage came upon him, and like an uncaged beast, he pounced at one of the men, throwing him to the ground. He rained punches of fists on the man's temple, severally. As blood stained his knuckles, unknown to him, a similar rage enthralled the others. A bloodbath ensued, with men tearing each other apart!

Below Steve's senseless punching, the man was dead but he kept beating on him like a bag. Then, a quick swipe of a metal rod on his back sent him spiralling to the floor, once again falling to blackness.

Steve woke to a bloody scene. All the men were dead. All apart from a writhing Kelvin. As soon as his movement became apparent, it was clear that Kelvin had set his eyes on him. He ran madly at Steve, grunting and heaving.

Steve felt for support, quickly hoisting his bloody body, feeling the ground on his feet again. Kelvin's eyes wanted blood. The air turned hot, and the confrontation turned intense as blow after blow was exchanged. Kelvin was losing his stance to a chesty Steve, wallowing off.

Before Steve could claim his dominance, Kelvin was up again, in his hands, a metal rod–the same one that had thumped Steve out cold earlier, "I have wanted you dead since the moment we got here!" In what seemed like a final rally of the bloody fete, Kelvin swung the metal with all his might. Steve duck from it. The rod clanged loudly upon striking the wall behind Steve! So hard was his hitting aim, that he fell, hands free of the metal.

The resounding vibration echoed to the core of each man.
Then, like a man from a deep slumber, Steve snapped out of it,

"What–What has just happened here?"

Behold, only two lasted!

One on his feet, the other nursing the burn on his hands lying pr-ostrate on the ground.

In the middle of their shocking awakening, the screen on Steve's arm came back. He looked at it, falling back to take a breath.

"It must have been the radiation!"

"What did it do to us?" Kelvin's hands were feeling hot tucked between his legs. Steve looked back at the dead bodies around them. "I am not sure...I think it turned us against each other. It turned us into some kind of..."

"...Animalistic neanderthals?" Kelvin said, composing himself to sit back up.

Before they could exchange any further, a small blue cube, similar to the hologram, came up from beneath the ground. It sat right in the middle, just like the first.

"We have to get out of this nightmare!" Steve said.

"Are you saying what I think you are saying? This happened right after trying to pick up the first..."

"Kelvin! Things around this place only seem to move when we alter with these random cubes. Whatever is in this place must have been testing us. We are the only ones that have survived. If we stay here, who knows what it will do to us..."

"Steve–you must be sure this time. I...I don't want to wind up dead!" Kelvin distanced himself.

"We have to figure out what's happening here. That box is the only thing standing in our way. We have to try!" Steve slowly stood, leaning forward towards the cube resting in the middle of the ground. Kelvin's eyes were peeled, swallowing hard.

Steve took a knee, looking at Kelvin–who shook his head in disapproval. 'Focus Steve. There is no other way.' He put forth his finger, feeling the top of the blue radiant.

Alas! It was real!

He gave a foolish smile to Kelvin, who eased his throat, sighing. Steve then picked the cube up, and immediately, the doors of the hall were raised around them, open! Then he exclaimed, looking back at Kelvin, "This is now the power box."

CHAPTER 04

Otis woke up in a daze to a piercing light. He shielded his eyes, n-oticing the stained glass pouring in the immaculate yellows, blues and greens. He felt the soft leather sofa he lay on. 'Wait...'

He sat up slowly, rubbing his eyes. The pearly white walls, 72-inch TV hanging before him, the polished mahogany table–'This is not h-ome.'

The obsidian black screen flinched, and the foggy chattering bec-ame clearer at the mention:

"...Cracks going as far as 50 Kilometers have been reported as a result of the quakes witnessed Tuesday around the Menengai Crater area. Government experts suspect that these were the signs of volcanic activity beneath the crater, one that was earlier thought to have been dormant for the longest time..."

Otis's face was not fazed, zooming from the news lady and back to inspect the opulence sitting around him. The impressive hangings on the walls–the pieces looked antic! He slowly stood, eyes up to the crystal chandelier hanging above him. 'Must be worth millions!'

He was so distracted to see a well-built man stroll in, glass and juice in hand.

"Ah! You're finally awake," He poured the rich yellow into the glass, its sweet scent filling the room. "Juice?" He lifted the glass at Otis.

Otis felt his throat. His tongue was like a dried towel, yet, "Who are you? How did I get here?" The man brushed his questions, walking straight at him. Otis backed up his hands in protest.

"Sit down. Hear what I have to say first," The man proposed, keeping a good measure of distance. He saw Otis eye the glass in his hand like a thirsty cobra, and took a sip, "There, it's not poison," He offered it, and Otis took it, still suspicious. "I am sorry for how my men got you here. We needed to be sure you were not being followed. We took care of *everything*."

Images of his abduction flashed past Otis's eyes, but then, the voice of this man was as calming as a breeze. So far, he had not died. So Otis took a first sip that quickly turned the glass empty. The man, noticing his thirst, pushed the rest of the juice his way.

"I am Peter. I have work for you," the man said.

"I don't take jobs from thugs. All I want to know is how I can find my mother and father..."

Peter remained silent at Otis's response, his eyes were blank. Otis walked around the sofa towards a huge fancy double glass door leading to a large balcony. The silence persisted, until, "I can help you find your father."

"And my Mother?" Otis asked, concern high in his heart.

"The men who took your parents felt that you might have seen something at the site. Something–dangerous, Otis. They possibly thought you were a threat to their operations. They wanted to finish the job..."

"What does that even mean? Just tell me where to find them and I will be on my way."

Peter's voice rose. "Otis, your reckless curiosity got you involved with some very dangerous men! Listen–the deal is, you work for me and you get to see your parents again…" Otis turned to a statue. Peter eased up the temperature, "…I promise."

Peter crossed to the front of the room, cutting through the tense air between them, and pointed at the TV. Immediately he stood near it, images filled its frame. On it, images of men in camo. He explained, "I am working under an organisation that protects African culture from infiltration."

Another image came up, "This is when we went to retrieve an ancient artefact in the deep jungles of Congo."

"Where do you take these artefacts?" Otis asked, keen to hear.

"We usually give them to the museums, others we hide far away from human reach. Some very bad men…uncouth fellows are after these trophies for profiteering."

"Profiteering, huh? How do I know you are not with those *bad men*? This you do must come with such lucrative benefits. I mean, it looks like you've done pretty well for yourself too…"

"…I have my means of getting compensated. I don't have to steal," Peter cut off Otis. Seeing his answer did not satisfy, "My father left a tidy sum from his investments. I was an only child," Peter's eyes stopped at the centrepiece sitting in the middle of the room. An older, gallant man wearing Peter's face sat in its frame.

Another image came up on the screen showing a group of foreigners in chains.

"As I was saying, many of those men are not from around here. Since the *Mzungus* came around, we have seen shiploads of artefacts sail to their museums overseas for their gain. This theft of our culture persisted in the shadows, even escaping law enforcers; until my men and I stepped in to curb them." Otis walked around the Sofa, "I don't understand. Looks to me like you have all the muscle you need. Why me?"

"Well, I actually find it admirable–how you went after the men who wronged you. Most people sit it out and pray. I follow something. A word my dad once told me when I was about your age. He used to chin up and crush me in between his arms and say, *'Bravery isn't the absence of fear. No. It is, many times, doing it anyway! Doing it afraid!'* You see Otis, when I heard about you, it reminded me of those very words. You embody that heart, you know–very hard to find! You fit perfectly with my crew!"

"...Okay...And is your group government approved?"

"All you need to know is that our operations are within the confines of the Law..." Peter's phone rang. Otis's eyes caught a glimpse of Peter's smartwatch. *'A private number?'*

"Excuse me I've got to take this," Peter walked out of the room, past the kitchen door. As Otis craned his neck, Peter came back looking distraught.

"Anything the matter?" Otis asked.

"Mnh–I..." Peter started, deep in thought. "I just got confirmation of the work I was telling you about."

"What work?" Otis was confused.

"The work..." The screen flinched again as Peter sat on the adjacent couch, showing satellite images of the site where Otis had sneaked to days earlier. Peter saw Otis's face, "Alright Otis, give me your word and we've got ourselves a deal."

"Then I won't be coming alone–Just so you try to double-cross me..."

"Do you understand the risk of this?"

"I have lost everyone I care about. I wouldn't suggest anyone else if I didn't think they were capable. Allow 2 of my friends. I trust them with my life. This kind of thing is really up their alley..."

"You're overpromising now," Peter stood up, stepping away.

"Noon. Tomorrow. The road to Menengai. They must not be late."

A cloud of dust arose, swiftly approaching the site's gate. Four black *Chevies* stopped at the entrance, boasting incognito plates. Out first was Peter and another man, dressed in suits. Then Ivy, cocky, flapping her blazer in the wind, "I've never felt this comfortable in a suit!" Ernest and then Otis followed. Out of the other car, men in black suits all followed closely behind Peter.

Ahead of them, the site guards took a position. Peter confidently showed a police badge. 'Just how connected are these people?' Otis wondered.

"This is private property. You cannot enter without..."

"This?" One of Peter's men came forward bearing a search warrant, then he handed it over to him. He showed the guard who took his time scanning the warrant, then nodded his head and moved back to the guard's room. "You understand he must make a call before he opens the gate, right?" The other guard taunted a suspicious Peter. The two remained silent, eyes locked. The other guard mouthed to the phone, his eyes still on the gate. After a while, he returned, "Give the guys at the controls a minute to open the gate."

Ivy was unsettled, "This is scum! They're buying time." Peter turned back to her and whispered, "Act professional."

"Are you friends with the police too?" The guard referred to the trio. Peter's countenance turned sour, "Do you think I'm playing here?" Again, the stare-down persisted in utter silence.

Before the exchange became more uncomfortable, the gates cracked open, much to Peter's relief. As he marched past the guards, he boasted, "We are the government. At some point, you've got to let up. Next time, make it less with the questions." He proceeded to the site, quickly succeeded by his men and their gear, with Otis's trio behind. On entering, Peter couldn't help but notice the odd stationing and layout of the place. 'Something is off here'

From afar, a white man came briskly at Peter and company, "Officers, to what do I owe this visit?"

"This is now a government matter. If you've got nothing to hide, you can be at ease."

"Well, what's to see here? It's a barren rock!" The white man said, realised nothing was stopping the unyielding Peter. "I can sue, you know. This is private property!"

"You don't want any trouble with me now, do you?" Peter showed his firearm, annoyed by his antics. "No. No trouble at all..." The white man stepped back, watching Peter's waist. He then walked past him, his interest vested in the cave revealed the further he got within the site.

Otis was on the other side, frantically moving from tent to tent. Ivy and Ernest followed behind him, concerned, "You need to relax." Otis rudely responded, "How can I relax? These people must pay for what they did to my father. Something has to give. I am only getting started!” His zeal only raised more questions for his friends.

Peter stood at the cave's entrance. It was deformed, falling apart after the quakes. *'This cannot be of natural cause...'* He inspected the large cracks. 'Must be an explosion.' He looked around, noticing electricity cables coiled back. *'Power? Yet no workers, just guards?'* This baffled him the more. He put his head in the darkness. It felt like a large cavity buried under the cave. He rolled up his sleeves, opening the latch bracelet of his smartwatch. He stepped close, carefully using his foot to feel where the cavity began to slope. He then lit his watch, throwing it within. As he was watching the watch as it dropped, he was startled, “What are you looking for?”

Peter jumped back astonished, to meet a confused Otis, “What have you and your friends found?”

“Nothing. They must have wrapped up a long while ago. It's like we are seeing what they want us to see. Something in those tents–I cannot quite wrap my mind around.”

Peter looked back at the cave's ruin, staying there no more, “I agree with you. Something really fishy is going on here. C'mon, I need to get eyes in there. We don't have much time.”

Peter brought back his men to the cave, “Do you smell that?” Ivy followed, “It is coming from the cave.”

“Right!” Peter exclaimed. “Bring the drone. Something's down there and I need to see what it is.” Immediately Peter took the remote to the drone, sirens marked the area. Armed police flooded the site, marking the men with guns and outnumbering them 3 to 1.

Otis took a step behind Peter shaking, asking in a low tone, “I thought you had a government licence."

Peter replied, "We can talk about that later."

CHAPTER 05

At the police station, Peter stood quiet but confident. His muscle of influence showed immediately when his lawyer arrived. Soon, they were free to go with a word from the constable, *"Mtu anasemanga mko na nani!"* The three friends slowly walked towards the station's gate, a little bowed. "First time, huh?" Earnest asked a shaken Ivy. A night at the cell was enough! Otis reached Peter, "Impersonating Police? You said to me your organisation was government-approved!"

"I am not that giddy about it either Otis, but I have done this work long enough–this is part of it. I got you in trouble. I got you out. No fingerprints! You are clean!"

"Can I trust *a thing* you say now? Is this part of your plan?"

"Otis..." Peter put his arm on his shoulder. "...That was my mistake. I promised you to get your parents back. I believe we are close. You have to be patient with this. " Otis looked at Ivy, and she concurred.

Then, a newly minted *rover* hovered right next to them, its double doors sliding open at the touch of a button. Peter turned to the three "Are you going?" Earnest choked at the ask, as Ivy held her jacket tight. 'How much money does this guy have?' A reluctant Otis watched his friends disappear within the velvety interior without flinching. Peter added, "You know, you don't have to come. Either way, you are already committed to this and only I can get you the access you need to see this through…" He walked to the front, opening the co-driver door. "The choice is in your hands."

Otis being heavily set on his feet knew no other way. He had been at the station once but ended up black and blue. This time, not a hair on him was harmed. He got in, the doors shut, and they drove off.

In a lab, the power box was cased in a glass chamber. Scientists observed it, examining it with tender precision trying to study its components and theorising on what it could do, potentially. Then, footsteps were heard entering. A white man in a suit walked straight to where the chamber was. Quickly, one of the scientists handed him a tablet explaining, "It seems the power box is made of a material that's producing the negative energy around it." The white man scrolled on the analytics, then asked, "What does that mean?"

"This right here is the future!" The scientist's eyes widened at the box. "Time travel…wormholes…A power much much ahead of all known science! The alien down there must be from an intergalactic civilization!" This was however not met with such excitement from the white man, whose eyes shifted to the power box.

"*Alien* power, huh? You do understand that this is the most wanted thing in the world right now. Your work here is done. Safely pack the box. We are going to proceed with the tests elsewhere, where resources are not as thin. We are taking this over now." As soon as he finished, another suit entered.

"Who sent you here?"

He raised the phone in his hand, "Here."

After a brief exchange, the man turned to the scientist, "You heard me the first time, didn't you? Get moving. This has to leave the country ASAP!"

Back at Peter's mansion, there was a rush! Peter led Otis, Ernest and Ivy beneath his staircase to an obscure button on the wall. The wall succeeded in sliding open to a dark room. Peter walked ahead, the lights coming on illuminating the expanse of the vast arsenal laid out in such intricate detail. The three stood in awe, baffled at what they were witnessing. Ivy could no longer hold her tongue. "What–Who are you?"

Peter had already reached a drawer at the furthest end of the room, bringing back a selection of small rounded weapons. "I want one for each of you. This is strictly for your protection, and for that only!" Once again, Ivy and Ernest took their choice, leaving Otis.

"There's no time. We have to move now, or lose our only chance to redeem this mission."

"Otherwise..." Otis made Peter's nose heat up. Ivy nudged him, and Otis slowly took up his weapon. Peter turned back, starting towards the distant drawer. "They're nothing dangerous. Just don't touch the middle button. Can you handle that?"

"What does this do?" Peter looked back to see Ernest exploring weapons set on the table behind him. He rushed to snatch it from him.

"Not all weapons here are safe!"
Otis asked, "Why do you need all these, then?"

Peter gave him the look from earlier. "Sometimes these missions get difficult. We make sure we are prepared in case of any eventualities. Don't touch anything here without my permission." He finished, his eyes on Ernest. He proceeded to bring back bulletproof vests, one for each of them.

"Wear these at all times. You are my crew now. Your lives are a priority to me!"

"Now what's next?" Otis asked, fitting his vest. Peter led them away through a tunnel way, out to the reveal of a sleek black car. Ernest marvelled. "Is that a *Maserati*!" much to Peter's smirk.

Two black SUVs zoomed past the busy downtown streets in broad daylight, halting in traffic. They shared much similarity in how they were driven, their windows tinted black. 'Escorts.' Inside the cars, were heavily armed men. In the first, Steve - *one of the men at the edifice searching for the power box*, sat in the co-driver seat. Suddenly Steve's phone rang.

"Where are you and why is it taking so long?"

"We are stuck in traffic."

"Why don't you use another way."

"We don't know another way."

"Ok, I will send you a new route right away."

"Ok!" Steve replied, hanging up. A text message beeped in Steve's phone. He looked at the message and said, "Turn left 100 meters from here."

Before the driver could make the move, a knock came on his window. Slowly, he lowered the window. A hawker carrying some fruits and juice leaned in, asking, "Matunda? Fresh from the garden!"

"No, we are all good," the driver came rudely, ignoring the guy. The hawker nagged, "*Chukua tu. Ni* healthy! *Hamsini Hamsini tu na hii jua...*"

The driver started closing the window to shut the hawker out, but before it sealed a metal slid through falling on his lap. The driver jumped, catching the rounded metal and grabbed the hawker's shirt. "*We! Hizi ni vitu gani unaangusha hapa?*" Steve caught a glimpse of it, waking from the baking heat in the car. "Wait, that's a weapon! Throw it out, now!"

The driver's red eyes met Otis's, reeling him into the car, disposing of the weapon out to the roadside. There sat Otis like a fish out of water, between Steve and the driver, surrounded by the other armed muscles. "Boy, who sent you here?"

Otis felt a cold metal pierce his back, his tongue swole as sweat cascaded down his *hawking* shirt. "Speak, or your body will be cold in seconds!" Steve pressed his chin. Otis stammered. Before he uttered anything fluent, a frenzy broke out! Suddenly, the driver's head swayed, spraying blood and a tooth on the dash. Before his heavy torso could swing back, Peter yanked Otis out through the car window with one arm. In a split second, the occupants of the car were left with no Otis!

Outside, Otis and Peter broke into a sprint. Steve jumped out of the car and started chasing them. Oddly enough, none of the other men followed to apprehend the two. Otis and Peter ran and entered into a sports car, parked a few meters behind the Escort, where Ernest and Ivy were waiting.

Immediately they entered the car Peter pressed the screen on the dash, "You can now open the traffic jam."

Ivy came from the backseat. "Did the plan work?"

Otis responded, "We still don't have the power box."

"We switch to plan B," Peter said, turning on the engine. He had a last glimpse of Steve who was running towards them. Wheels screeched, as they sped off! Steve pressed his ear. "Follow that car!"

After a meandering drive street after street trying to lose their chasers, Peter slowed down in an alley. He looked at the rearview mirror to see if they were followed. Relief. "The coast is clear," Peter assured the three, driving out, eyes peeled.

As they backed out, Peter heard a shriek from behind his ear. "Watch out!" Beside them, two black SUVs veered off the junction running over hawker's wares on the streets, ramming through cars parked by the road. Peter, in a quick reflex, drifted his sports car 360^0 facing the chasers. His palms held the leather of his steering wheel, narrowly skidding off to a corner feeding the road the chasers were on. On seeing this, one of the assailants cussed reaching for a gun.

"No guns, remember? We are foreigners here—we cannot do anything to blow our cover." Their driver warned in such a heavy Dutch accent.

Otis turned to Peter from the co-driver's seat. "Why did you turn?" Peter, with eyes glued on the road, responded, "I wanted to know if the car carrying the power box was the one chasing us. It wasn't the one."

"Don't tell me we are going back for it?" Ernest asked, with shock on his face. Peter didn't answer him, turning to a busy merchant's street, losing the chasers momentarily. He turned to Otis, "Do you know how to drive?" Otis was lost of confidence, stammering, "Aah—a little bit..."

"Hold the steering wheel and drive. Keep away from the highways. Stick to these back routes."

"What—Why?"

Peter turned to Ernest. "Yeah, I am going back for it!" Immediately, Peter opened the car door ignoring the concerned screams behind him. "Don't do it!"

Otis forced his weight across the cabin to the driver's seat, leaving *matatu* drivers and conductors on the road bemused.

Otis felt the steering, struggling to take control of the slowing car. 'Feet on pedals, hands at 3:45.' Loud honking behind them startled him. "Otis, can you drive this car?" Ivy questioned him.

"Sure, sure. Give me a second..." He looked down at where the pedals were. "Eyes on the road!" Ernest shouted. "Okay!" Otis felt the steering, controlling the car. He stepped on a pedal, and a loud Rev came from the engine, pushing the car ahead. "Ah! That's easy."

Ivy rolled her eyes, "Peter better come back, and quick!"

Otis noticed his friends' dismissing tones, "C'mon guys! I've got this..." He noticed he was running out of road. "Why again are we not supposed to go to the highway?"

"I don't know. Perhaps Peter knows you can't handle his car on a speedway." Ernest came.

"I think–I think we can try," Otis was getting pumped up about the experience. "Ki-*James Bond*, eh!" He looked at Ivy in the rear-view mirror. She was not impressed. "Just do what Peter said."

"*Kwani mnaona mimi ni kurutu aje?*" Otis stepped on the gas pedal, the car accelerating into incoming traffic, onto the highway.

"That's how you do it!"

"Otis!" Ernest shouted in his ear, "...*Karao wa Traffic!*" He pointed at the traffic cop on a bike signalling him to park by the road. Otis shrunk into the leather seat, pouting in angst. "If you just did what Peter said. Now what is this Otis? Man!" Ivy complained.

As the cop marched past the car, adoring it, yet eager to apprehend the driver. He knocked on the window. "Jesus!" Otis felt a shiver in his back, lowering the window.

"*Afisa...habari yako?*"

"Young man?" The cop stepped back. "Is this your..." –comparing the car with those abode.

"Why are you overspeeding?" He assumed as much: spoilt politician kids.

"Officer, I was trying to save my life. We are in danger..."

"*Wacha Stori mingi*. We know you. Where is your driving licence?" The cop was serious. Otis knew better not to pretend, but as it was, he'd rather look like he had lost it. Behind him, Ivy and Ernest sank in their seats, silent. He was on his own. "Get out of the car." Otis obliged.

From a distance the chasers watched all this unfold. As Otis walked out of the car, one commented, "Where is the big guy?" The driver bit his lip, then clicked his tongue. "He is after the power box! He must have known we didn't have it."
Immediately this was clear, they drove off, leaving Otis to the cop.

Steve got a call.

"Where are you?"

"Relax. I am well on the Expressway!"

"The man we were chasing is not with the boy."

"Wherever he could be, don't lose that car!"

"It looks like we lost him amidst our chase. Check if anyone is after you?"

Steve sluggishly peeped out of the window, only to see a motorbike roaring beside them, with a gloved hand throwing a canister to his side. It started gushing out white gas, "Tear gas!" Steve lost control of the wheel, crashing through the barricade, flying off the highway, overturning with a smoking defaced engine. Besides the crash, a surviving hard case.

Peter got off the bike, and walked towards the case, picking it up, and feeling its weight. He clasped it tight in his hands and rode off on the bike. Steve was down, strapped in his seat belt, marking the face of the rider. He felt his head, freeing himself to exit the crash, crawling out of the car.

The other SUV arrived on the scene, moments later, the men attending to Steve quickly. "He took the power box!" He grieved, cussing out loud.

Peter felt his phone buzz while riding away. 'You've got a call from an Unknown number?' He picked up, hearing a thin voice on the other end.

"Don't listen to them..."

"Otis? Where are you? Are you guys safe?" Peter stopped at once! A deep voice followed, **"If you want to see them again, bring the power box NOW to this location."**

"What location?!" Peter demanded. His phone buzzed again. He quickly checked to see the coordinates on it. Then, the caller hung up.

CHAPTER 06

The dim bulb was all the light in the room Otis, Ivy and Ernest were left in by their assailants. They were barefoot, tied up to metallic chairs littered across its wet floor. Otis raised his head, turning to see if anyone else had come to. On his right, Ernest was knocked out, deep asleep. 'How can he even sleep at a time like this?'

He turned to his left and saw Ivy seemingly unfazed. He remembered the events that led them here. How after a brief confession of his crime, the cop had asked them to trail behind him to the station. Briefly down the highway, a truck separated them with Steve's men hijacking the arrest, orchestrating a diabolical yet stealth plan. Otis swerved to the left to avoid a collision, only to end up on the wrong exit, where more men were waiting to ferry them away in that same truck. *'Ki-James Bond, indeed.'*

"How are you holding up?" Otis asked in a low tone. Ivy did not respond.

Otis sulked, looking away. He continued, "Do you think Peter will come for us? It felt like that power box was all he needed. I can't stop thinking...what if we were just collateral damage? Perhaps we weren't supposed to..."

"You know what Otis—just shut up!" Ivy cut in.

"Ivy, I am just trying to...I am worried for all of us."

"Worried Otis? You are the reason we are here in the first place!"

"But everything I did back there was to get us out of this situation. Now you are blaming me?" Otis burned.

"And here we are! We were doing just fine, Otis, following Peter's instructions. But no! You had to be the hero, and for what? All he asked for you to do is to keep off the highway..." Ivy's temper heightened to silence.

"You were well aware of the risk of doing this. They were spelt to you word for word, and you agreed to it. I didn't force you in..."

"Tell me again, why is it that it is us you called for this? Why are you always like this? You've been ignorant your whole life!"

"So it's like that?" Otis's voice became shaky.

"It's like what, Otis?" Ivy asked, looking away.

"The way you said that–Ivy, we have been friends ever since we were kids. You knew I would do whatever it takes to keep you safe. I saw the look you gave in the rearview mirror. I saw your eyes. Sure, I got a little carried away, but I want to make things right..."

"Then make things right, Otis. You do not have to impress me or Peter or anyone for that matter. The Otis I know can be reckless sometimes, but he knows when to stop and think. You are better than that, Otis. This is no childish game. It's real life, and people could die."

"Well," Otis swallowed hard. "I guess people change. Not everyone gets it easy like you..."

"Easy?" Ivy came at Otis's comments.

"Yes, easy! Not all of us get a silver spoon up our mouths. Some of us have had to go through things...oh, why bother? You wouldn't understand anyway."

Ivy turned to Otis, a tear blending out of her right eye. Her voice was heavy with emotion, unsparingly chiding Otis, "Why would you even say that? All the years you were out and about winning school trophies...overachieving. My parents made sure I heard all about it at the dinner table. Asking, *'Why aren't you like Otis, Ivy?'* To them, there was no better example of a child...Do you think it's easy to always be compared to someone else? Living in someone's shadow, yet your best cannot even stand next to them in any way! And to think I even considered a future with you..."

Both Ivy and Otis went completely quiet. Otis looked down. The guilt of his actions ate him up. Then he softly cooed to a sobbing– "Ivy..."

A loud *clang!* Came from the door. So loud, it woke Ernest! A man walked in, straight as an oak donning a tailored suit fitting to his wrists and ankles, tight upon his neck. It felt, almost, as if his presence made the room's air thin. He smelled of death! Behind him a guard with an old black metallic box. He inspected the captives, stopping at Ivy. He took out his thumb caressing her wet cheek, "Young girl, this is not the place for the soft of heart." Ivy spit on his suit, "Go to hell!"

"Whoa!" Ernest was taken aback, exclaiming to his side, "Someone's feisty."

The man gave a creepy smirk, leaning towards Ivy, "I like your guts. I am Lennox. What's your name."

"My name is none of your business!" Ivy barked at him.

Lennox gave a dry laugh, turning to where Otis was. "Tell me. Where is your leader hiding?" Otis caught the scar on Lennox's eye, spanning to his ear. Grim and grizzly, "I–I don't know."

Lennox stretched his hand to the guard, still focused on Otis, "Bring me the tools. We will start with the girl." The guard quickly unlocked the black box, to unveil a set of crude metals, tweezers and what looked like gardening secateurs. Otis looked at Ivy, noticing her eyes widen in fear. "No, Start with me!" He defended, tensed. Lennox took out a towel from inside his jacket, wiping his hands, "Trying to be a man? We'll see about that." He freed his left hand, his skinny fingers dancing on the tools as if feeling which one would be more torturous than the other.

He took up one, a dull cobbler's needle. It looked like it had been buried in tetanus for a long time. He faced down Ivy, "You will tell me everything I want to know. If I ask you about what you ate last Tuesday, you will tell me. Do you understand?"

The three shook in their chains. Otis felt the cold unbreakable ropes on his arms, holding his breath, 'What would *James Bond* do?' Right then, another guard dashed in, straight at Lennox, whispering in his ear. The news did not seem to amuse Lennox. He firmly lifted the needle above Ivy, twisting it in the air, then calmly said, "It seems your saviour is here. Pity. We could have had so much fun!" He then walked out of the room with the guard, leaving the other manning it.

Guns were cocked, men in line all aiming at Peter. In his hand was the most coveted item, the briefcase lost in the crash. His lower back rested on his lost sports car, his eyes shone a confidence that in a sense withered the threat before him. Then, from behind the line of fire Lennox mocked this staredown, walking right between the guards and Peter. Still, not too close to where he was.

"I never thought you would come, let alone bring the briefcase."

"You said this–in exchange for my friends. I kept my word, Lennox. It's time you kept yours."

"Ah! You even know my name. Let's skip introductions then," Lennox snapped his fingers, and one of his scientists appeared from behind the guards, screen at hand watching it like a sniffing dog. "Fool me once, did you? But, you cannot fool science." The scientist neared Peter, then to a halt came hastily back to Lennox. "It's got to be it! The energy radiating says he's got it!" Lennox looked pleased, sliding his hands back into his pockets.

"I have to see them first," Peter interjected. "Oh, they are fine. Believe me. Though, if you stayed a little longer...this could be a whole other story."

"I want to see them," Peter demanded. Lennox turned and said, "Follow me." Peter tightened his grip on the briefcase, following Lennox with no further questions. The guards kept a high alert, pointing at him even as he walked towards them. "Relax boys, he is now a friend," Lennox directed the guards, who in turn lowered their guns.

"Acting tough won't help you," One of the guards manning the room teased Ivy.

"Go bark at another tree. I have had enough of this place!" Ivy was hostile.

The man came down to face her in the eyes. "Let me tell you something lady, but let me tell you something, you're not getting out alive. I know my boss well, he does not play games."

Ivy eased her demeanour. "Now that's more like it!" Suddenly, the guard was struck from behind, falling unconscious. Otis stood above his body with a metal leg from his chair at hand. He paused, his entire stance pointed at Ivy, who locked eyes unable to turn away. Ernest's croaky whisper cut in, "Otis, be quick before they come back!" Something about that brief moment made little sense to free them. But Otis was fast to action, unfreezing himself to untie Ivy first.

The more Peter followed Lennox through the endless maze of the building's corridors, the more he felt clueless about his plan. He stood by it in his mind– *'No letting the briefcase go until he recovered the three.'*

He looked at Lennox's unwavering lead. Something was off. He stopped. Lennox walked a few steps ahead, then noticing only his steps were echoing, "Is that briefcase too heavy?" Before Peter could answer, a taser went to his spine, bringing him down stiff. He couldn't help his body, as a man built like a mountain jumped over him sliding the briefcase to Lennox.

"The guts to come here on your own. You don't expect the Lion to stay jaws shut in his den now, do you?" Lennox gave a smile to his side, snapping his fingers again. "Show our friend here exactly what I pay you for!" The mountain of a man turned to Peter, fist to hand, as Lennox menacingly vanished beyond the corridors with the briefcase.

"The first ones won't hurt. But slowly as the *stingray* wears off, you will beg me to end you!" True to the man's words, the dragging and strangulation were not felt. It was the first punch to the stomach, following another to the ribs that woke his system up. Wallowing to the ground, he felt a little strength in his legs, pivoting his body on the wall. Another punch followed, continuously rocking Peter's temple. The man saw Peter flattened to the floor, standing up to wipe his hand of blood with his shirt. Before he could finish, Peter felt his toes, quickly swiping the man to the floor with his leg. The man crashed down like a sack of potatoes, unsure of what hit him!

Peter bounced back, pulling up his shirt, ready for a man-to-man. "For such a puny man, you pack a..." Peter cleaned the expression off his face with fistfuls of pain. The man shoved Peter away, as he staggered to his feet. Peter looked to see the corridor's end to see where Lennox had disappeared. He felt his pockets, realising that he had lost something. His eyes looked where he had fallen, to see a small device resting there. 'Sometimes, you've got to go through mountains.'

He bounced off the ground, throwing an elbow to the man's sternum, kicks to his triceps and punches on his ribs. The man grunted, shaking off the pain to grab Peter's arms, headbutting him to the head then spearing him to the floor squarely. As he intensified his offences on Peter, his rage suddenly caved to a resounding hit on his head. He fell to a great thud, moving to unveil Otis's silhouette in Peter's shaky view. Peter slowly rose from the ground saying, "I had him...right where I wanted him." Ernest was amazed at Otis, "You're definitely getting a medal for hitting people's heads today!"

Peter marched past the three as if nothing had happened, taking up his device from the floor. Ivy asked, "What is that for?" Peter responded, pressing the controls. "I could not trust their word..."

"The target is too far off your radius."

Peter cussed at it. Ernest asked, "What is that supposed to do?"

"I implanted a bomb into that briefcase, just in case they double-crossed me. They are too far for me to activate it," A frustrated Peter kicked the floored man so hard that his belly wobbled from the impact!

Lennox drove off the vicinity, almost flying off into the distance. "Have they all died?" He spoke to the speaker in his car.

"We are not sure of it."

"Detonate the bombs."

"But some of our men are in the building..."

"This is a command! Detonate the bomb."

"Ok, boss."

Peter led Otis, Ivy and Ernest back the way he had been led. He looked sure about it, but after each turn, it almost felt like the building renewed its corridors. Right then, a series of *BANGs!* followed from behind them, each taking to the floor.

"What was that?" asked a panicked Ivy.

"Those devils want to blow this place up!" Peter said, getting up. He felt the wall beside him, noticing a flaw.

"Quickly, this way! This building is about to cave!" Peter ran forward, Ernest following. Otis slacked waiting for Ivy to catch up.

"C'mon!" Then, the flaw turned into a big crack and the floors started trembling.

"You two, hurry before it's too late," Peter looked back, holding the door out of the floor. As quickly as his words came out, the floor started breaking into half. Ivy slid deeper in, looking at the ruins of the floor above them. Otis reached down to hold her, lifting his other hand only to feel a metal bar sticking out of the fallen wall. "Grab hold before it sinks!" Ivy felt the floor drag down and leapt to grab onto Otis as the floor disappeared into the rubble.

Peter saw this and quickly pushed Ernest through the door, headed for the emergency stairs.

"Will they be alright?" Ernest asked, fear in his voice. "I should have listened to you. I should have stayed home!"

"You're here now! Man up and help me save the others," Peter said, running down the staircase like it was a slide.

Otis's palms got sweaty as Ivy's weight dragged on.

"Don't let go!" Otis prayed in his heart to make it, but his arms were weakening fast. Ivy fixed her eyes on him, desperate but holding on. Then, another *BANG!* followed, shaking the metal Otis hung on. He looked down to see a single standing concrete beam right beside the rubble.

"Ivy, you've got to jump!"

Ivy in bated breath looked down, her eyes marking the fall.

"JUMP!"

Eyes closed, life in the air, Otis watched Ivy vanish in the dust-filled air below them. His arms were tired immediately. It is like he had only strength for Ivy. He slipped off the crying metal, and closed his eyes, 'Here we go.'

Peter and Ernest ran down the staircase, shielding their heads only with their hands, as the floors above fell. On hitting the landing a floor below, two large concrete lumps sat before them blocking their supposed exit.

"What do we do?" Ernest panicked. Peter looked around as if finding his soul. Then—it read on the wall, on a tiny ripped plastic hanging, '1st Floor'.

"We are only on the first floor, Ernest..." He moved back, spotting a broken glass window on the Stairwell's side. "...So?" asked Ernest.

"We can jump out!" Peter said casually, clearing some rubble off the floor. Ernest's face drooped. Peter looked down.

"C'mon. There is nothing much we can do about them...It's the only way out!" Ernest felt the rampant shaking increase, as the floor above them cracked. He quickly gestured a prayer running to where Peter stood, both rolling out of the building.

Otis looked up and saw the columns slant. He shook his head, getting up on his feet to see Ivy a distance off.

"Otis, we need to get out, now!" He smiled at her. "Quit fooling around!"

He followed Ivy on the column, as the path ahead cleared to the balcony on the next building! He hurried, pushing Ivy yet firmly steadying her to the end of the column.

"Only one way out..." Ivy said hoping.

Otis nodded, holding her hand tightly. As the floor above them creaked and sagged, they jumped off!

Peter stood near Ernest, who was in great disbelief atop the roof of the sports car parked right beside the building.

"We-jumped-off-a-building!"

"I must say...we got lucky. They usually crumble on the first explosion!" Peter said, head low, coming off the van's roof. Then, a surprisingly soft voice caught him from behind.

"How did you guys get out?"

Peter turned to quite a shock! "You…You made it out?"

With a grin, Otis dusted his shoulders, "This, you've got to hear!"

CHAPTER 07

Night fell quickly, and in no time News about the building's collapse was on everyone's feed, including the 7 O'clock News:

"I am standing right outside what was a 6-storey building under construction, here in the outskirts of Nakuru City. Witnesses heard several loud bangs coming from this area, leading to the unfortunate incident late this afternoon, causing a massive power blackout in a 30 KM radius. Initial forensic reports indicate that explosives may have been used in the falling of this building. There has been no comment from the well-known owner of the building, who has since gone into hiding despite several calls for arrests from locals citing that the demolition was possibly a terrorist attack. They reported an increased presence of foreigners in the area in the past few days. Still at large are the alleged perpetrators, whose faces were identified after CCTV camera footage was retrieved by the Police. We would like to bring attention to the public, if anyone may have the whereabouts of this man believed to have led the operations, to forward information to the nearest Police station..." On the screen: a diabolical face of a man, with a vicious eye-to-ear scar.

At one of the police precincts around the city, the news was coming in hot! In one of their holding cells, sat a frivolously roughed up woman. On seeing the bulletin with the man's face plastered all over, she quickly sprang up, pushing her head into the metal bars as far as it could fit.

"Hey!..." She shouted across the dingy hallway where she was kept at the first sighting of an officer.

"Here! Let me get to my stuff. Get me my phone–I can arrange for what you asked for..."

A male officer came to her cell, "*Sasa umekaa huku hizi siku zote? Eh?* People can talk!" He dangled the cell keys at her face. Her eyes were not on him, but the glaring headline behind him. 'I am coming home, Otis.'

That same night at the airport, Lennox sat in the Lobby. His left hands were hidden under his jacket, next to him–the briefcase. He lifted his head to the announcement of his flight. He smiled to his side, spotting Steve at a corner, who took quick strides to the immigration desk. As Steve took care of their documents, something unsettled Lennox. He felt an unnerving cold dig on his hip to the right. He turned to see a straight face daunting him.

"You thought you'd get far?" Immediately, Lennox looked down to see a pistol at his side. "Get up. We don't want to start a fuss. You are under arrest!"

Lennox's face remained unfazed. He turned to where Steve was and saw another man confronting him. "It seems you came prepared..." He stood up as urged by the plainclothes officer. They began to walk out the Lobby, Lennox exchanging a glance with Steve. He then turned to the man arresting him.

"Mind letting me go to the bathroom first? See, you're a good man. I can tell by your sense of duty, and how you love your, what...3 year-old?

You don't want to get in the way of the people I work for..." The man did not respond, pressing him further.

"Fine then. Don't say I didn't warn you."

While edging out of the Lobby, two gunshots were heard:

"EVERYBODY DOWN!"

The officer pushed Lennox down, turning to see where it came from. Then, all around marked men remained standing, guns at hand. Without warning, gunfire roared, pelting bullets at the exposed officers and airport security. The officer dodged the razing fire, jumping into cover beside the lobby exit, leaving Lennox on the floor.

Immediately the gunfire ceased, he got up frustrated, lifting his head to see if he could spot Lennox, Steve or his partner. They all had vanished!

"Check for casualties!" He instructed the forthcoming backup. He then ran down the escalator to check the lower deck. There at the airport's Taxi-way, he saw Lennox looking straight at him with a wide grin on his face. The man lifted his sleeve, "Suspect is attempting an escape. I repeat Suspect is leaving the airport now!" He shoved his way past the flocks of tourists and travellers. On getting to the Taxi-way, he saw two black SUVs drive off. He pointed his gun, shooting at the vehicles...'Bulletproof?'

Then, the second vehicle opened its back door and falling out was his partner. His back hit the tarmac hard, as the door shut and the two vehicles sped off leaving every security apparatus in utter confusion. He put his gun away amidst the pandemonium running to tend to his partner.

Lennox sat in the back-left seat in the first SUV, furious. He took out his phone, lashing out at Steve who sat in the co-driver's seat, "What was that?!" Not expecting an answer, he continued to compose himself making a call, "...We've bumped into a little bit of a problem. I wanted to borrow a plane this evening. I hope that's not going to take away from your convenience. For business, of course."

Peter's car slowed down at the curb, up the road towards Ivy's place. It was a long quiet drive all the way. Peter looked back at the three.

"Here you are." They alighted, all looking tired and worn.

"You did well today. Go rest. We're done for the day."

Ernest leaned towards the car window, "I know you feel the heavy responsibility to shield us. We get it. But, we are not kids here. After today, I think you can breathe easy now. At least we didn't die." Peter did not share the same expression as Ernest. He remained grieved, "All in a day's work securing our culture, huh?"

As they walked away each in their direction, he rolled up the black window and sighed. He stopped for a second, then tapped on the screen at the dash. It zoomed off the driving controls, displaying a myriad of videos of the airport from different angles. He double-tapped on one of them, showing two SUVs driving off. He paused the video, rewinding it and enhancing the image to catch the plate. 'Got you!' He closed the tabs, keying in the details on the plate and suddenly, his destination changed, a red dot blinking hot on the screen. He then drove off the street, disappearing in the thick darkness.

Otis dragged his feet, unsure about returning to his house. Despite Peter's reassurance, he still hadn't kept the promise. He had known it would take some time. What bothered Otis was the feeling of being watched always. Before they parted, he had considered asking about lodging with Ivy or Ernest, but the trouble would be too much especially because of the way their day had turned out. He figured it was better to go back and clean up the house.

As he approached his place, he noticed something odd, the lights were on. He started creeping for the fence, eyes peeled. He heard sweet humming and a delicious scent floating from it. 'Mother?' He wondered. He picked up a thick chunk of firewood, then slowly, he approached the door, and alas! It was not locked. He looked around, and just as Peter had said, the mess was taken care of! 'Maybe not...'

He followed the trail of fresh jasmine and cinnamon towards the kitchen quietly, his palms pressed firmly on the wood. He peeked to measure his offence, only to see, "Mother!"

Otis's mother turned to see her son. Undignified, she dropped everything running to greet him. They both fit tightly in each other's arms, tears and joy flowing all at the same time. Otis did not think he would ever miss someone this much.

"Where were you? Did they hurt you?"

"Otis, my son...I am okay!" Otis's mother got off her tiptoes after the lengthy hug. "Go take a shower. Change from these awful rags–I am making your favourite! Come down and then we can talk, okay?" Otis saw the sheer fondness in her eyes, nodding his head reluctantly. He didn't want to get his eyes off her lest she disappear as she did the last time. Before he could bolt off, something beckoned.

"Who cleaned up the house? I left it a big mess!"

Otis'smother hesitated, "Oh dear–I found it neat already..."

"I thought you...But really, mom. Where have you been? I have been looking all over for you..." Otis's voice didn't shake a bit.

"Well, if you must know now, here…" She dragged out a kitchen stool for Otis. Otis walked back, picking up a diced carrot to chew on and sat.

"When we left the station, I tried to call you several times. I had no clue where you were…" her voice cracked. "Your father's work was a secret he kept from all of us, even myself. That day, I got a message. An anonymous tip that our lives were in danger. *They* told me to run as soon as I could, Otis…"

"Run? Run where? Did you tell the police?" Otis got concerned, sitting up.

"I did. I thought it better to abandon everything, and since you were not answering my calls…The police offered to book me in for a night or two in their cells until the threat had subsided. I got out today…" Otis saw how she wrung her fingers. "Wait wait wait. All this while you were with the police, in a cell? You didn't think to text me at least?"

"Otis, there was no other way…Plus, after our argument back there, I didn't know if you could trust a word I'd say."

"But mom…Even a simple text? I mean—wouldn't it matter to you more that I am safe?" Otis rose, his mother following, "Otis. You don't understand…"

"Tell me what I don't understand, Mom. Spell it to me like I am a child. Am I even…" Otis held back his words.

"The police said *they* could be tracking my phone…I made a choice. Regardless of it, here you are—would it not have mattered to you to calm your anger and just pick up my calls? I too was worried sick!"

"So now it's my fault? If anything, it sounds like I did the most work to try and keep this family together. You have no idea what I've been through..." Otis responded, fuming.

"You got us in this mess the first time when you went looking for your father's dead body at the site!" His mother's voice rose.

"No one was giving us answers! You didn't say a thing, and neither did the police. What was I supposed to do? Be home and hopeless? Did you even Love him?"

His mom was stumped at the question, turning her back to Otis. "I loved that man through some difficult times, Otis. But some secrets were not worth dying with..."

"Secrets?" Otis asked, following her to the kitchen counter.

"Yes, Otis. You are a grown-up now–and if you didn't hear it from me..." She turned to look at Otis, "...You have become the son we hoped for. I know that from my heart of hearts, I have always and will always love you, but your father and I have had many fights over the years about this. I figured it is best if I...Otis..." She swallowed hard, as Otis's confused face persisted.

"Am I even your blood?" He asked, taking a step back. His mother shook her head slightly, tears flowing again. "Explains why he punished me so much. How could I not see it!" Otis stormed out, and she pursued him.

"You were so little then. We applied for the adoption process, and all we wanted was a child we could raise as our own. Otis, I was the best mother I could be..."

"Yet you couldn't stop the beatings? You saw him force me to sleep hungry...what kind of a mother–No! You never really loved me. Keep your tears. My whole life, all I wanted was to be a good son to you. Yet you...You left me here, on my own. Just like it didn't matter when *he* died, huh? I don't need you—and you know what? This..." Otis picked up a picture of the family and broke the frame. "Congratulations! All your eggs are in the same basket now. You got what you asked for! How selfish could you be?" He slammed the door behind him, leaving her weeping deeply on the floor.

The cold air outside failed to come down the wrath in Otis. He heaved in both pain and disgust. 'Everything I've known is a lie! Everything I cared for!' He went up the hilly rise at the back of the house, up the terraces that are the foot of Menengai. He sought solitude there overlooking the night sky of Nakuru city. He watched blankly as headlight after headlight flashed down the road, his mind as distant as distant could be. He sat there, not knowing who he was anymore.

"Otis?" A voice called from the other side of the Terrace.

"Over here, Ernest!" He waved, cringing over the unwanted company. Ernest climbed to where he sat.

"Maybe it wasn't the best idea to go home straight. I mean, after all that's happened."

"No. Actually..." Otis helped him up. "I found my mother...she is back home."

Ernest felt a hint of lament in his words, but, "Okay. Great! Glad she is home. At first, I thought you were angry we didn't ask to host you, especially Ivy..."

"Please, don't start. Not now..." Otis came.

"Fine! Fine!" Ernest said, reaching into his pocket.

"You know, after today, it's not the same anymore. Like, don't you miss that adrenaline of not knowing what's going to come next! Being on

the edge of danger, standing close to the flame and not getting burned–
that kinda thing!" Otis turned to Ernest.

"Tell me I am not the only one looking forward to that again..."

"Way ahead of you," Ernest flaunted a thin touchscreen. "Don't
judge me yet, till you hear what I've got. Here," He lowered it for Otis.

"Peter said he was done for the night, right? He lied. I got this–okay,
stole it from him, back at the building collapse. The man's out on a
pursuit right now. Any guesses?" Otis shrugged his shoulders at Ernest's
ask. "I think...he is going after Lennox. I got home and found my dad
watching the news about some airport shoot-out. They said it was
connected with the events of earlier. See, the same face! Peter is headed in
that exact direction, right now!" Otis smiled a little, as Ernest continued,
"Looks like adventure is back on the menu, Otis! Are you ready?"

"You're not planning on leaving without me now, are you?" They
were both startled, slowly turning to meet Ivy standing right behind
them.

CHAPTER 08

In the guise of the night, Peter drove to a halt parking his car a few meters off the road leading to where the red dot on his screen had stopped. He sat there for a while, planning his entrance; he needed to convince himself that he was doing the right thing going at this alone. So far, he had chosen to keep his covert team out of this, and he wanted to keep it that way. Finally, he decided.

He walked to the boot of his car, changing to all black. He then moved stealthily up to the clearing where could see the gates of the premises. He went around, outside the barrier of concrete and mesh surrounding the private airstrip. He spied on any activity. Then, he saw the numerous armed men littering across the airstrip. *Lennox's men. He's got to be there.*

He unzipped the side pocket on his pants, swiping out a tiny monocular. He saw some of the men pack up cargo in one of the planes sitting outside the only hangar there. *They're getting ready. I've got to hurry.* He got up, but then more commotion followed. He watched again to see three youngsters, hands tied up, being frogmarched by two soldiers at the crosshairs of his monocular.

"No. No. No...I told them to stay home!" Confirming the faces of

Otis, Ernest and Ivy, he threw the monocular in anger, "This complicates everything!"

Otis was at the front, then Ivy and then Ernest. The three were led to the hangar, guns pointed everywhere they turned. 'This was a bad idea,' Otis was sweating through his shirt unsure of how they would get through this. He regretted putting up Ernest to steal his father's car to follow Peter; He regretted putting Ivy through the fence, almost twisting her ankle on her way down. Anger had gotten the best of him: *false confidence!* He thought about Ivy. *'Collapsing buildings may be slow, but not bullets...'*

Then, "In a line!" a crackling bass came from behind them, each following without question. "On your knees!" It commanded again. Before their buckling knees could follow, boots were breaking their stand at the knee, shoving them to the hard concrete. Ivy yelped. Ernest gave sobs of despair, but then. *"Mwanaume unalia kama dem?* SILENCE!" It became pin-drop quiet.

In a split second, the men realigned, stepping out of the way to reveal Lennox. In his hands, the solitary briefcase. It cracked in his grasp, as he hit his head with the butt of his pistol.

"You three have been like a thorn to me! A bad itch!" He faced them, putting his pistol down. "You want to be a hero? Do you even understand what you are chasing? This...You won't even know what to do with it if I give it to you! Am I the only person who sees that *he* is using you?"

He stepped forward closer to the three, "Why do you want to risk your lives for nothing? Listen..." He shook the briefcase. "Tell me, what is in here, huh?"

"I..uhm...a powerbox?" Ernest stammered at the ask.

"Yeah, but to power what?" Lennox barked at him, to no answer. He waved his pistol, giving out his dry maniacal laugh. "They have no idea what it does– *haha*! Why are you chasing it then?"

"It's illegal what you're doing!" Braved up Otis, "You are stealing from our culture. It is ours to protect, and we will..."

"You will what? Huh?" Lennox gave a cold stare at Otis. "Let me educate you, you ignorant kids! This here is ancient energy. Not even your ancestors in their best witchcraft could plant such power underneath the soil! Even I don't know where it came from! Now, I need this energy because it is exactly what we require to get us through many many projects. Life-changing projects– the kind that changes the course of humanity. What do you Africans know about that? You didn't even know it was here in the first place! I dug this out with my money. I know where to put this into use...but you are standing in my way, and I do not take that kindly."

Guns cocked, aimed at the 3.

"I know you're there..." Lennox raised his brows slightly. "I am giving you 2 minutes, or these three are done!" He licked his lips expecting.

Then, out of the pitch blackness outside, a woman's hands lifted. Behind her, an armed guard pushed her at gunpoint. Otis froze.

"Boss! Look who just showed up..." Irene, with a face awash with tears, walked into the light. "Ah! Remind me your..."

"You Killed Jeremiah!" She whiffed.

"Yes! Jeremiah's wife!" Lennox signalled her forward. "I didn't kill Jeremiah, didn't you hear? There was an accident at the site. Tony was buried underneath it. Now, he read the contract and these are normal things in operations like the one he was working at. It was an act of God...he was a good employee."

"You heartless..."

"Me? Heartless? For all I know, there are things in this world that take– courage, I would say. Not the kind to go through fire, no. The kind that will do everything it takes to alter the very fate of humanity. Your son here..." He pointed his pistol at Otis, noticing him hung his head. "Does he...wait, you told him! Spares me the time to have to break it to him...Otis here thinks that you can just reverse the river. He thinks that everything in this world is broken. What people like you don't understand, is that no one owes you anything. Good people die every day, and for what? Does it change a thing? No! I am one of the few still willing to look at grief and pain and take it on to see a greater good achieved!"

"Even if it means to kill people?" Ivy choked at her question. Lennox quickly turned to her, "Don't be naive! No one, not even Peter does what they do for free. We all risk something! I am the only one willing to accept that that's how it is. Everyone sells to the highest bidder, isn't it so, Peter?"

Peter appeared from behind the hangar, Steve's head locked in his arms, "Drop your guns, or I shoot!"

Lennox smiled, turning to meet Peter's entrance, "There you are. The other half of me! However, did you manage to escape the building…"

"Shut up and let them go!" Peter pressed, as Steve grunted under the pressure of the gun on his temple.

"What? No need for the briefcase?" Lennox taunted. "We all want the same thing here…"

"The kids…or he dies, now!" Peter was determined.

Lennox glanced at Steve, then back at Peter, "Alright. No need for violence when we can talk. Let them go. Let's see how this *one man* plans to save himself."

Immediately, Otis felt his hands freed. He stood, much to the embrace of Ivy and Ernest who urged him to exit the scene. His eyes did not abandon Peter, who nodded at him to follow his friends.

As the three neared where Irene was, they saw her sulk, "You don't have to forgive me, Otis…" Otis walked right past her. Ernest held her hand, as she followed behind the three, whispering, "You two can talk later."

"There! They're gone…" Lennox put down the suitcase to take off his jacket. "It's just you and I now. Give up! You are outnumbered!"

"No. These men you have here–they are men under oath. They are to protect this soil as much as I do." Peter continued.

"Power, Peter. Power does not care. I can buy anyone if I want! Like I said, everyone sells to the highest bidder…"

"Exactly!" Peter said, throwing Steve to the ground, and opening fire!

"What do you think Peter is doing?" Ivy asked Otis.

"I think he's buying time…I still can't figure out how he plans to come out with the briefcase." Otis replied.

"So, are we going to leave him there?" Ernest asked, to which Irene answered. "I came all this way so you guys can get out of danger. This is no longer your problem!"

"She is right," Ivy recommended, afraid for their lives. "We are just a bunch of youths. We bring nothing. There is nothing we have that could make a difference for Peter, really. Like, we survived once already! This is not the kind of thing I am willing to stand in the way of. Let Peter handle it."

"I don't think you two understand. Peter risked everything to keep us in his team. There must be something about us—not what we are but perhaps, we are not here by accident..." Otis started. "We owe it to Peter to try and help salvage the situation..."

"To death? How Otis?" Ivy asked plainly.

"Exactly! To what end?" Irene supported her.

"Fine then! You go ahead. Me and Ernest will go back and help Peter..." Otis pulled Ernest from among the ladies. "Are you with me?"

Ernest hesitated.

"Fine! I will go. After all, Peter came to me first. I might as well end up with the one person who saw something in me," He stomped off, towards the hangar.

Right then, gunshots erupted!

"Otis!"

Peter took cover behind a freight truck, as the gunfire intensified. In the cover of the chaos, Lennox and Steve, like a pack of foxes, took up the suitcase with the powerbox, running off towards the Plane sitting outside the hangar. Lennox's last command being, "$10,000 for the one who brings the body of that man to me!"

CHAPTER 09

Bullets enraged flew over Peter's head, where he hid. He composed himself, aware of what was at stake if he delayed. The men came closer, "There is no way out!" Peter glanced at the hangar's roof, seeing the first rays of day pierce the dark. He made a silent prayer under his breath. It was almost as if his soul wished to leave, but couldn't. As if he desired death another way, but this was it–the end.

Otis fell on the ground flat. Ivy was screaming uncontrollably, as Irene held her. Ernest was in shock, mouth ajar! Around them, the pitch black began to clear as day broke. Then, more gunfire, "Get Down, now!" Came a commanding voice behind them. Ernest turned to see men in military gear surrounding them. Quickly, the men yanked them out of the line of fire, drawing them to the side of the hangar. The one leading the pack of about 15 elites signalled their silence. Ivy could not hold herself, "Otis!"

Otis lifted his head slightly from his prostate position. He saw the battle lines thin for Peter and lifted his body slightly. Before he could crawl, he saw the men in the shadows and knew to wait patiently. 'The Cavalry has arrived!' He heard Ivy scream his name from across the yard, lifting his head again. One of the elites rolled into action, taking up the range between Otis and the shoot-out in the hangar. "Go! Now!" Otis rolled out of the way into safety, running like a survivor to where Ivy, Ernest and Irene were waiting. "What were you thinking?" Ivy asked, grabbing hold of him, and tightening into a long hug. He shrugged his shoulders, still shaking from what he had seen, "So you do care…" He then felt a second embrace, that of Irene. It hadn't changed. *Still smells of jasmine and cinnamon.'*

Peter heard the rain of bullets fade, and the trudging of boots come his way. He held his gun tightly as if it were his own life. He watched to his left, his eyes manning the coast. The first guard crossed his line of sight. He shot at him, and the guard's knees buckled as he fell to his death. "Anyone else who crosses that man will suffer the same!" He warned, his voice more gutsy than brave. He looked back and saw the body being dragged away.

What followed was a series of even louder shots, marring the hanger!

Peter fell, his head between his arms, unsure of what was to come. Then, a sudden ceasing, as the hissing of a plane rose in the back.

Lennox had seen the men coming, rushing into the plane with Steve trailing behind him up the aft door. In his right hand, the briefcase and the pistol in his left. Lennox gathered new momentum as he walked past the cargo of machinery, marking the closure of his operations.

"Open the door!" He bullied his way into the cockpit, finding a disoriented pilot sitting on the controls. "You…Fly this thing!"

He pointed with his gun, frustration clearly outlined on his face.

"Bu…But my co-pilot…He's not here yet…"

"Do you think I care?" Lennox's eyes widened. "You fly us out now!"

The pilot turned to the controls, starting the engines, "Alright, but we will have to make a stop around Douala. The plane will need refuelling..." He heard Lennox take out the safety in the gun, quickly pulling the brakes, and increasing the plane's throttle.

Peter heard a pair of confident steps approach. He eased from his cover, to meet a pair of military pants beside him, "Are you okay, boss?" He breathed with ease, slowly rising to the warmth of the peering sun.

"Thank God you came!" The officer from the airport lobby held Peter's arm, shouting atop the roaring plane engine, "Go! They're almost gone. We'll handle the rest..." He led him past some wounded bodies on the floor.

"Otis, Ivy, Ernest..."

"They're secure sir!" Assured the man.

"Okay," He looked at the edge and saw more of his men. He became slightly calm. He increased his pace towards the clearing, "I need speed!"

"Take my bike. If you hurry, you can still catch them!"

Steve rushed to the cockpit, "Shut the door! That fool is coming for us." Lennox turned, his face like he had seen a ghost. He shouted at the pilot, "Close it!"

The pilot hesitated, "I need to fly this plane right, please put your gun away...I have a family..."

Lennox was getting impatient. He had thought about it, but then– he shot the pilot, his body wallowing off the seat, falling off.

"What have you done? Who's going to fly the plane now?" Steve panicked. "Go pull the lever up. It's already moving, isn't it?"

Lennox fixed the briefcase beneath his feet and threw the dead pilot from the seat, occupying it. "We fly, regardless!"

Steve put his hands on his head, confused. He had his orders. He walked down towards the plane's tail as the wind beat his chest, he stood at the door's end watching Peter valiantly ride right behind them, swift as a kite!

The door started lifting, as Peter gained on the Plane. He looked ahead, noticing that they were running out of runway. He clenched his teeth, standing on the bike, planting himself for a launch. Steve felt the screech of the front wheel as it raised off the runway. The door wasn't closing fast enough.

As the plane began to lift its nose, Peter knew his chances were thinning and he couldn't wait anymore. He took his chance, hitting the brakes, catapulting his torso in the air, flinging him past the closing door's thinning barrier and crashing into the fuselage.

"I hate your guts!" Steve cussed, walking towards Peter's fallen body. He reached down, grabbing Peter's shirt from the back. He raised him, throwing him across the cargo boxes, hitting his back on the wall. Peter groaned, yet to recover from the fall. He shook his head, catching the growing approach of Steve's body in the corner of his eye, "You should have stayed down!"

Steve grabbed Peter's neck, hammering his knees into his ribs continuously. Peter fell, coughing dry air as the pain seethed to his bones. "You cannot win!" Steve boasted as he manhandled Peter, holding him up to render further punishment.

Peter felt the plane climb sharply, quickly grabbing hold of the safety belts on the cargo, as Steve slipped off the floor hitting the back of the plane.

Peter steadied himself on the plane floor.

"I am not here to win. I am here to make sure you lose!"

He went forward, meeting Steve's face with his boot. Steve spiralled, hitting the floor with his knees. Peter reached for his gun.

"Any last words?"

Steve raised his bloody eyebrow, slowly cracking a smirk. Then, Peter was hit hard from behind, losing his gun and falling to the side. He writhed in pain, looking up to see Lennox stand above him with the briefcase at hand.

"This is as far as you go, you tick!"
A defiant Peter held out a tiny remote.

"Not if I can help it!" He pressed a button, and the briefcase lit up red, exploding into a shattering fireball on Lennox's chest!

CHAPTER 10

"....warnii...warning...Warning...war-NING!...WARNING! WARNING!!"

Peter woke to a loud, blaring noise resounding in the red-lit cargo hold. He felt resistance–like a heaviness was holding him down. He opened his eyes to blackness. Surprised, he wriggled seeing red light peer atop the black that covered him. He was hidden behind a large wooden fragment. 'How did I–' He pivoted his arms, revealing the turmoil within the hold. He looked around to see a charred piece of metal, in their midst, a smoking body. *'Lennox!'*

Groaning came from his left. Steve sat up in his hands, a shimmering silver cube securely strapped to his stomach. He looked across to where Peter's frame was appearing. He dusted the burning pieces on him, latching onto the charred mess heaped around him.

He felt a sharp pain in his left leg, still, he insisted on crawling to the lever up top. He used his weight to see the aft door re-open. He leaned on the wall, as air rushed through the cracking, a parachute on his back. He looked back to where Peter was grinding against the wooden fragment, trying to inch out, "...Stay down!"

Peter looked on, fighting to be free of the weight holding him. He watched the door as it widened. He heaved to make room to free his legs, but with every push, his energy lowered. Suddenly, the plane hit turbulence, moving the fragment slightly. *'He wants to crash this plane...'* He intensified his struggle to be free, with renewed zeal.

Steve held on tightly as turbulence shook his stance. He was determined. The box was a priority. The door gapped wide open, and he moved closer to the exit. He turned, only to miss Peter where he had last seen him. He cussed under his breath, pressing forward quickly to make a jump. Right then, a weight thrust him hip-first past the plane's aft door, plunging into the cold air behind him. He was freely falling to another's weight; Peter's.

They wrestled mid-air, tussling. Peter hammered on Steve's back, as Steve grabbed his pants to throw him under. Then, Steve looked below to see the ground approach! Just missing the tandem attitude, Peter detached from Steve as he deployed the parachute on his back. Peter, missing a strap, dived to grab Steve's left ankle, straining Steve's injury. Steve's response was kicking to rid himself of Peter, only for him to hear the silent dash of a bullet cross near his ear. He looked down, to see his gun pointed at his face.

Peter pulled the trigger without thinking twice. He held onto the hanging body, overlooking the plane nose-diving at a distance, crashing in the background. He looked down, as the distance between him and the ground thinned.

A wide-open field awaited...

For a second, Peter felt faint. He felt the sudden brushing of grass on his face, freed of the suspension that floated him to safety. He saw Steve's body crash, atop the shimmering silver box. He thought to rest, rolling on his back exhausted. *'I must be crazy or something...'* He felt the warmth of the sun, taking in deep breaths. He gave a weak laugh, sitting up. *'All in a day's...work?'* Something rattled the ground.

Behind him, the plane's crash had already settled–*'What gives?'* Immediately, he looked to see Steve's body melt at the increasing activity of the powerbox. Then, a burgeoning current ramped up out of the powerbox bundling him further away. It bolted up the power lines, sparking flames on the masts around the wide-open area.

Ivy's eyelids flickered. Her curled eyebrows gave way, as she took in a breath–the air was tainted with bleach and a faint under scent of blood. She raised her head, tilting it on her shoulders to her left. "Otis?"

Otis rumbled from his sleep, underneath a hospital blanket on a couch. He rubbed his eyes, noticing Ivy's smile.

"How long have you been there?" Ivy asked softly.

"...the whole night," Otis yawned.

Ivy sat up in her hospital gown. "How's your back? Mine's killing me..."

"...and you had the bed? This couch–I might never recover," a brief chuckle came up in the room.

"Thank you..."

"For what?" Otis asked Ivy. "What you did back there. That was..."

"Reckless?" Otis looked away.

"...You could have died! But–brave," Ivy smiled again.

"There is a thin line. Peter once told me, "Being brave is showing up scared.""

"He did, huh? Wasn't that a movie, or something?" Ivy said getting off the bed, a cast on her left hand. She saw Otis stand to help, but she waved him down.

"Sucks...but it's not that bad. It's what I get for trying to save the world..." She put her weight on her feet and then walked up to where Otis sat. "...I sure hope Peter is fine though." She saw gloom come upon Otis. He did not look fine for a moment.

"He is a proper hero. I don't know how he does it. Like–a real-life *James Bond*!"

Otis scooched over, as Ivy sat next to him. He felt her lean into his chest, prompting him to lift his arm around her. They sat there for a while, quiet, Ivy nibbling on her right thumb as Otis smiled down at her, "You know, I think we made a great team back at the collapsing building."

Ivy's body turned, "Do you see yourself with Peter? Like, doing this work long term?"

Otis brushed off the question.

"I am serious, Otis. I cannot count how many times he's put our lives in danger–the past 2 days have been us running to no end..."

"Ivy, I also learned in the last 2 days that my entire life has been a lie. That the two people I thought I had, weren't even being truthful with me at all. I'd rather keep Peter than roam around with papers being nobody to everyone."

"Really? A nobody?" Ivy got up from resting on Otis's chest. "Why must you be so difficult to everyone? Irene was just trying to protect you..."

"From what, Ivy? I–I can't..."

"Otis, I think the most important person in your life right now is the very same person you let down each time. And he is sitting right in front of me right now," Ivy stood up, shaking her head. "Ern and I have followed you to death, and do you know why? Did you even consider why we would say yes to a stranger's request? You are that reason, Otis. We trust you. You mean so much to us that we have followed you to hell and back, but you still want to bury yourself in bitterness and all the choices people made in the past! Does it occur to you that they too made a choice? Irene could have let you! They could have chosen–I don't know, another way...but they still made room for you. You had a good life. Perhaps, even as you move forward you should let her be in peace."

Otis remained quiet. His eyes did not move from Ivy's slowly welling up tears, "I didn't realise that..."

Ivy proceeded to sit back next to him, "Who cares about what you are or not, Otis? You still have my vote...you still have a friend in me." Otis quickly brushed his cheek with the blanket to rid it of the tear dripping halfway. "I am sorry, Ivy. I–I have been a little too selfish with the way I have treated you. I cannot see myself being a proper friend. Friends don't let each other risk everything they have. Forgive me..."

"I already did, Otis," Ivy consoled, looking forward to the flowerpot right by the window. She smiled with such glee, "Whose are those?"

Otis snapped back to his normal self. "Uhm...Irene and Ern couldn't stay the night. They left early. Peter's men and some cops waited until everyone was cleared, then took them home. I insisted on staying, but they'll come for me in the morning...So, Irene got you some flowers. Jasmines. Her favourites." He chuckled. "I can't believe she carried those in the car all that while."

Ivy walked away to the window, feeling the radiance of the fresh buds and petals, "This is the best hospital stay ever!"

"Why? Cause of the flowers?" Otis teased her. She glanced at him, "Well, that..." She came back giving a cheeky dance. "...and also the fact that you chose to stay. That was so sweet of you." She sat back next to Otis, much to his delight, "So, you do care..."

Before she could cosy up next to him, something taunted Ivy, "Otis...tell me something. I saw–at least, I think...back at the airstrip. I thought I saw you get shot..."

Then, there came a noise–a shriek from the room next to them. They stood alarmed, listening.

"The power...It went off!"

"The machine is not working...I think we could lose him!"

A hurdle of nurses came rushing out of the room, side by side a bed with a patient. Then, lights in their room flickered to blacking out.

"What do you think is happening?" Ivy asked an equally astonished Otis.

"I...I don't..." Otis stuttered reaching for his phone. On holding it up, it shocked him. He quickly threw it on the hospital bedding only for it to fry.

"I don't know!" Otis said, looking back at Ivy.

CHAPTER 11

Outside, one of Peter's men stood waiting.

Otis turned to Ivy, her face quickly dampening at the happenings, "I know...you've got to go."

Otis bit his lip, unsure whether this was the right time to leave her. He felt her hand abandon him, "Go. Save the world." He felt a guilt about it. He wrestled within, while still aware of how significant everything happening outside of their little world was. He helped her back on her bed, his promise to return written all over his face, and then he took his leave.

Where the Powerbox sat, nothing else remained. It had flattened the ground with constant pounding. Meters away, the sole survivor, Peter hid behind a fallen aeroplane fragment, trying to escape the heavy electrical charge in the air. Then, it calmed. Peter had lost every electric thing he had on earlier. His monocular, his pager...everything.

It was then that the ground began to rev, like some heavy thing moved by. He rolled to see a large mechanical marvel. It was like a truck on gigantic wheels, joints squawking and metals crying. He watched with delight as one of his men came down the contraption, behind him, Otis!

The pair saw Peter wave them away from the powerbox, obliging without question.

"I thought we were supposed to come collect the box?" the man asked.

"What is he doing here?" Peter asked him, eyes sternly on Otis.

"I'm here to help. To make history..." Otis replied confidently.

"He insisted on coming. I figured, you already trusted him with this mission so far..." Before the man could finish, Peter erupted. "Him and his friends stole my tab! They came to an unsanctioned crime scene, putting the mission in jeopardy...No!" He turned to Otis. "Get going! This is far too dangerous. I–I cannot risk this. Not on your life. Not again!"

"After all we've been through? I–you came to me. Went through the trouble to get me to your place...remember the collapsing building? How you left Ivy and I..." Otis felt a pain in the chest.

"Exactly why I cannot have you around. You are deadweight, slowing me down! The game is over! Whatever part of the mission is left, is for the real mercenaries, Otis. You got what you bargained for now, didn't you? Your contract is done."

Otis looked away from Peter, and for the first time, he did not have a response. The man nudged Otis to go wait in the truck, then slowly went to where Peter sat picking up some of Peter's electronic gear. "He just wanted to repay a little of his gratitude, boss. He's done nothing wrong"

"I know that. He has seen too much. I only meant for him to be on one mission. One. Not the whole thing. I messed up!" Peter said.
"I always trusted your judgement. I don't doubt it one bit!" The man raised Peter from the ground.

"Well, we all make mistakes every once in a while..." Peter consoled himself, looking back at Otis who banged the door on the truck. "He is not ready yet. I got him through some horrendous things–I can't explain how he kept coming back, you know."

"Perhaps he too has your kind of heart. Now that he is here, it is a long way back. Perhaps you can let him know..."

"It will complicate everything," Peter held back a proper response. The weight in his heart was like lead.

"No one is ever ready. You weren't..."

Peter walked back to the truck ahead of the man. He hesitated, then pushed past his hesitation. He held the handle to the truck, and it felt hot but he pulled it anyway. He revealed a quiet Otis, surrounded by a barrage of manual levers and gears. Not a screen in sight!

"Sorry about earlier...would you come down for a second? I got uh– I've got to tell you something. Something important," those words crawled out of his pride, scrapping all the air in his lungs. Otis, like a good soldier, came down, following behind Peter to the back of the truck. He beat the gravel on his path, leaning onto the truck.

"There are things about our operations that I should have come clean about from the get-go..." Peter rubbed his neck. "We are not a government organisation, but we work with them. This–" He hit the truck with his hand. "We call a *Rig*. It is part of our research at Futuretech, where I am CEO. We developed these units for the military, in anticipation for such an occurrence." Peter alluded to the Powerbox.

"Futuretech? The electrical company?" Otis finally asked, to which Peter nodded. "So, the government always knew about the site? Why did they let the likes of Lennox in there?" Otis reiterated, more engrossed in what he was hearing.

"Lennox was not always who he seemed to be. At least, not in his first years working in the country. I met him at a mission briefing many years ago. His firm was chosen to lead the team in research around an anomaly around the Menengai Crater. There was big money poured in, and with it came certain conditions. As it is with most men at the helm of such operations, he who pays the most gets to have the say. He bent to their will, and quickly, everything was compromised. When the report on their findings was leaked to the rest of the team, a tussle began..." Peter paused, as a noise rattled from afar.

From behind them, more *Rigs* appeared from the horizon, painted grey and some camo. The man from Peter's team went ahead to meet the incoming company.

Peter was perturbed as two military men marched towards the, in the background a myriad of activities quickly set off. Tents were being set up, and equipment was being laid out.

"What are you still doing here?"

Otis, looking confused, stayed silent, while Peter replied, "Well, I have witnessed the advent of this...I have an idea to deal with the situation."

"And who exactly are you?" the military head asked.

"I'm the CEO of Futuretech. If you are well endowed with knowledge about us, you know that this is well within my jurisdiction."

"You are *the* Peter?" The General glanced at the crash site, then back at Peter. "You—you survived that? Why, you are quite something! I'll give you that...and still standing!" The General quickly switched. "...But this is no electrical misnomer. You can leave. From now on, this is a military operation."

"What if I have some valuable information to offer?"

Rudely, the head responded, "You have done your bit! We don't need anything from you," and turned to walk away. Before he left, Peter called out, "Project BC!" The head paused, then turned to the soldier with him and commanded, "Leave us!"

The soldier quickly left, and the head turned to Peter, intrigued. "Who told you about that?"

"I designed the project."

"You are turning out to be quite a package! Tell me something...must the boy stay during this conversation?"

"He's with me, and I trust him," Peter did not hesitate, much to Otis's confidence boost.

"Alright. I'm General John. Now, tell me what you know."
As they walked through the military tents, Otis asked Peter, "I heard you mention Project BC. What is it?"

"It's the name of the project I just told you about. I helped develop it with other scientists to address potential EMP effects in the future."

"EMP? I don't follow..."

"The moment the Powerbox activates, everything that uses electricity goes down—from cell phones to planes. But as you can see, some military vehicles are moving. Just like our *rig*, they run on mechanical engines. I believe they want to use that technology to lift the power box out of the Earth's atmosphere."

Suddenly, General John stopped in front of the bare field. A gigantic vehicle–a supersized Rig was being driven in, carrying a rocket. "This is our latest improvement from Project BC," he said.

The rocket was moved to a launch pad, and soldiers hurriedly prepared the area for flight. Peter, Otis, and General John watched from a distance.

Once preparations were complete, two soldiers in heavy heat-resistant gear approached the power box with chains hooked onto their backs. After final confirmations, one soldier crawled under the rocket and ignited the fuel manually with a flamethrower.

The rocket roared to life, creating thrust beneath it.

Everyone watched in silence, waiting for it to launch.

The rocket finally took off, lifting from the ground and the success of it brought joy to the military personnel.

As the rocket ascended, Peter felt his phone vibrate. He pulled it from his pocket and saw it was on. Before he could speak, a soldier rushed up to General John, exclaiming, "General, Project BC has worked! The lights are back!"

General John turned to Peter and said, "Well look at that. It worked!" He followed the soldier moving away, leaving the two. Otis gleefully turned to Peter. "You did it!"

"I'm still not convinced," Peter replied, not reflecting the same optimism as everyone else. Otis had seen how he had edged out everything the military had been working there.

"But it's done! That's great, right?"

"With that speed…it's still not out of our atmosphere—just out of our line of sight." Suddenly, a missile launched from another rig in the military camp.

"No!" Peter shouted, running frantically toward the control room.

Inside, he found General John and two soldiers at the computers.

"What have you done?" Peter shouted, reprimanding the General.

"That was a matter dismantler," General John replied unbothered.

"You should have let it go."

"We only removed the EMP field. It would grow over time. Taking it off the planet's orbit was not the solution."

"No. I did the math. There is a 5% chance that bomb will solve that problem…"

"It's a matter eater; it will completely consume the matter. It is a chance I am willing to take. Man of science, even if I had a 1% chance, I would take it without a second thought. That is the difference between you and me. You calculate, I act!"

Before Peter could respond, the computer beeped, and they all turned to see a countdown: 10 seconds until the missile reached the propelling power box! Peter bolted to the outside, bracing himself for impact.

The sky lit up with a red hue, followed by a loud explosion:

KAKRAAKK!

Everyone under the sound of it fell to the ground, witnessing what could only be described as the second coming. All eyes up!

As he watched, General John walked beside him, "Satellite images are back. They reveal that the box has been completely destroyed."
Peter turned to the general, his expression grim. "I told you, not everything in the universe obeys the laws of physics."

"But at least the EMP effect is gone."

Just then, the general's phone rang. He answered. The voice on the other end reported, "The scientists called it. The signs are there …we have only a few hours left before Earth experiences unprecedented solar radiation." This wiped off the smile on the General's face. He looked back to meet an increasingly uneasy Peter.

"I need to take a cold shower; I'm burning up for some reason."

The General came up behind him, "You're burning up because we have only a few minutes before the most significant solar radiation in history hits Earth." Peter paused, taken aback by the news. Hopelessness washed over him as he walked away.

The fate of the world was inevitable. Doom was coming.

CHAPTER 12

Underneath a flowering Jacaranda, on a bench outside the hospital, Otis sat next to Ivy. Both were sad and silent, but there was no better company. Ivy became fidgety, finally breaking the monotony asking, "So, we have counted Hours to live?"

"Minutes now, I think. There's nothing we can do but watch."

"But isn't this like, a global disaster? Why can't anyone...the *United Countries* or something–come to help us?"

"Yeah. At best, only about 30% of the earth can survive what's coming. The only country that has offered to fight it, even using the fastest jets, won't be here in time."

"But we should have hope...surely, it cannot end like this. All because of that stupid box we chased around?" Otis turned to Ivy, "It's not stupid, Ivy." Ivy sensed he was a little incensed. Otis continued, "I am here, not to discuss the end of the world–I am here to talk about us."

"Ivy, I'm sorry for the times I've ignored you. I know I've done things that make me less deserving of you, but I wanted to say this before the world ends: I love you. I've always loved you. I–I just couldn't find a way to express it because...Because I was afraid."

Ivy leaned in, kissed him briefly, and then pulled back. "You are the most brave person I know, and the past few days have proved that to me beyond any doubt. Otis, the world may die today–or maybe not, but whatever happens just know that I also love you. That if anyone could do anything to make the last day on earth something amazing, it is you."

Otis smiled, his eyes widened, and he felt his heart beat once more. "Well, since my folks were supposed to pick me up in like an hour, I guess...Peter?" Ivy called out, her eyes widening past Otis's frame.

Otis quickly turned, "Peter, Ern? What are you doing here?"

"I knew it! Took me a minute, but again, where else could you be?" Ernest teased, as he met Ivy and Otis. Peter lagged, speaking over their little reunion, "We've got to get going if we want to make any progress."

Ivy asked Otis, "Where to?"

"Where everything started. Peter got info from papers left behind by Lennox at the airstrip that there's a larger *thing* underneath the site at Menengai," Otis answered.

"What are you expecting to find back there?" Ivy asked, crossing her arms. "The missing piece to all of this," Peter answered.

"A missing piece? You only have minutes left! Shouldn't you be doing something better than putting your lives in danger again?" Ivy turned to Otis, thinning her eyes.

"That box must come from somewhere...I am willing to try one more time before I die. What if we end up saving the world?" Peter did not wait for another question, proceeding away from the three.

"Otis? You're going with him?" Ivy tugged on Otis's arm. He looked into her eyes, "I think you know the answer to that..."

Her heart frowned, but as they disappeared around the hospital block, she sat back, looking up at the burning sky. "You couldn't have ended a little later?"

Peter, Otis and Ernest arrived at the extraction site in Peter's rig, driving past the gates of it. This time around, the site was unmanned, fully abandoned. Peter, Otis, and Ernest walked into the cave, unsure of where to start. Peter checked his watch.

"We have only 34 minutes to try to save the world. You all had the allowance to say goodbye to whatever and whoever you love. It is now or never, boys!"

Peter rolled out the cable from the rig's bumper, fixing the headlamp on his hard cap, and began the descent into the dark abyss. Peter led the three down to the shaft that overlooked the burst hole leading to the edifice. They cautiously ventured deeper into the darkness, scanning their surroundings, ending up in a hollow groove. Peter instinctively poured light forward, as the two followed until they reached what seemed like a door. Ernest approached the tiling upon it, assuming the handle.

Peter quickly stopped him, saying, "Hey! If you make a mistake, we're all dead."

"I don't see another way through!" Ernest argued, stepping back. "Then what do we do now?" Otis asked, backing up Ernest. Peter moved closer to the door. "We move swiftly, but not carelessly." Ernest and Otis watched in silence as Peter examined the door. After a few moments, Peter announced, "I want to touch something, but I don't know what will happen, so be ready." He reached beneath the tiling, pulled it outward, and planted his wristwatch.

Then, a light beam shot out from the door.

"Lasers! Get down!" Ernest shouted. As the beam moved above them, He noted, "You can keep doing your thing while I stay on watch."

As Peter resumed his examination of the door, Otis called out, "Peter!"

"Wait! I'm close to cracking this," he replied.

"This cannot wait!"

Ernest turned to follow Otis's gaze and saw the laser beam moving rapidly toward them. "This cannot wait, Peter!"

Peter turned around just in time to see the mesh of the laser heading toward them. Quickly, he took out his phone, pressed a button, and struck it on the door.

"Everybody down!" he shouted, taking cover, as the watch beeped rapidly before exploding, causing the door to blow open.

As the dust settled, they looked on to see the opening upon the gaping door. Excitement filled Peter as he stood, "The door is open!" Otis and Ernest rushed past him, jumping past him, into the opening. Peter clambered off the floor as the mesh came quickly behind him. He leapt forward, seeing the burning laser burn his shoe sole slightly. Immediately he turned to see the mesh die, and the door closed as if the explosion had made no scratch upon it!

"What witchcraft?"

"It's not witchcraft Ernest. That's tech beyond us," Peter said, getting up, his eyes wandering all over their alien abode. He examined the floor. 'This is no metal...nor stone!'

"What's that smell?" Ernest asked, pinching his nose.

"It's coming from the left," Otis sniffed in the air, unsure whether to follow. Peter led them into a hall, and scattered upon the floors were several dead bodies.

"Whoa! Looks like a butchering fest in here..." Otis said. "Smells like it too!" Ernest came, burying his nose in his palms.

Peter took stock of what they wore, "Explorers. These must be Lennox's men...This is why we all must tread carefully." He continued to the middle of the hall. It was like he was looking for something. Then, neon-like lights grew from the floor's edge illuminating thousands of pods arranged systematically.

Ernest, instantly unfazed by the rotting flesh beneath his feet, and moved towards one of the pods, "I have seen this in a movie before. I think they're–*Aliens*?"

Peter reached into his chest pocket for a small card, stating, "Hibernation pods. So, yeah, alien–and there are lifelings inside too."

"I can't believe that this was here, underneath our home town all this while!" Otis exclaimed, wading past the dead bodies.

"This...ship must have carried a civilization many many years back. The question is, from where?" Peter said.

"Only one way to find out..." Ernest pressed, leaning in towards one pod curiously.

"There are thousands of them! If we start searching now, we'll lose time for our mission. I suggest we spread out and look for clues on how to stop the Powerbox." Peter said, scanning the hall. "There!"
He saw a similar tiling to that on the door. He fit his hand under it, and this time, with very little resistance it gave in. A pathway flashed out of the monolithic walls to what seemed like a control chamber.

A large mainframe sat connected to multiple terminals growing from the black, coral-like walls. The sheer size and make of it marvelled them!

"It is like it's from the year 3,000!" Ernest said, almost falling over gazing at the ceiling of it. Otis noticed what seemed like a seat and walked over to sit on it. He felt it, soft like a slimy leather. As he got comfortable, he felt a button on the side of the armrest and pressed it. Suddenly, strange rumbling noises echoed through the hall, capturing everyone's attention. Then the door to the main hall behind them banged shut, startling both Ernest and Peter.

"Sorry about that," Otis said, quickly being made aware of his error.

"What have you done?" Peter panicked.

"I did nothing, just sat down!" Otis defended profusely.

"Get off the seat before you bring us more trouble!"

As Otis lifted himself off the seat, he accidentally pressed another button, and his hands and legs were locked in place. He tried freeing himself. "I can't–guys, I'm stuck! Help me!"

"Stay still!" Peter instructed, worry curving on his face. Ernest rushed to Otis, trying to get him off. With every heave, Otis's limbs sunk in the seat more. Peter stopped in his tracks, noticing the walls collapse inwards. Slowly but surely, the space was shrinking!

"What should we do?" Ernest asked, breathing fast.

Peter looked behind, "The pods! Run to the pods, now!"

Before he could make a run for it, a crackling noise filled the chamber as fog filled the floor of it. Peter looked back to see Otis's desperate attempt to free himself. 'No. I cannot leave him again.'

He ran back, pulling out a thin blade, "I will dig you out if I must. If the world ends today, then we might as well go with it!"

Right then, the crackling stopped.

The silence grew more scary than the noise.

Whatever was coming was going to take them all alive!

Then, the walls paused. Otis looked up, to see the mainframe wake, "Look–"

The three stopped, frozen in fear. Peter dropped his blade, perplexed at the large black face poised upon them from what they presumed was a glass screen.

"I am *Lemma*. Venus is my origin. Not the Venus you know here on earth today." It began.

"Wh...what are you, Lemma?" Ernest hissed, afraid and shocked at the same time.

"I am a supercomputer created by my maker."

"Who is your maker?"

"Wait." It moved from the mainframe to a peripheral one.

"Sample achieved. You are a descendant."

Otis wondered at the robotic voice, "Descendant?" Lemma returned to the mainframe and explained:

"I have dwelt here on Earth for 8,000 years. I came here as the set coordinates to flee the planet Venus and to carry a future generation of The Black race by my Maker—the leader of that race, Floki. Africa was chosen to be the beginning point for a new sprouting for the race. You are children of The Black Race that I was designed to protect. He was indicted for irreversible damage done on the planet, before its end."

The three watched the mainframe as it showed Venus inhabited by an advanced civilisation, bearing skin just like theirs.

"Then...you must know all about this Edifice and its every function?"

"I do. I also noticed that my Powerbox is missing. I may not run at my full function."

"Yes, the powerbox–It has escaped to the stratosphere absorbing so much solar energy, it may deem earth unlivable."

"The box is made of negative energy. That is how it powered the ship to travel across the interplanetary divide and arrive safely."

"I want to know how to stop it before it's too late."

"Like I said, its absence means that my systems cannot fully run. You will have to do this manually."

"What do we do?"

"I will take one of you to a door where you can retrieve its catcher." Lemma released Otis, then:

"I choose you, KATO."

They were all taken aback, "Kato?"

"Yes," Lemma continued. **"I traced your blood to a prominent warrior at the heart of Venus's tribes."** Otis's eyes shone, seeing a brave face, standing in his posture on the mainframe before him.

"Lemma, we don't have much time left. Please, take him to the door," Peter cut in.

The left wall then curved out a passage shaped in Otis's frame so only he could fit. **"Walk forward."** The computer urged.

Otis looked back to Ernest and Peter, "Wish me luck..."

"Go!" Peter pushed him.

Otis rushed through the wall's opening, arriving at a cabinet as high as the ceiling, within it possibly thousands of drawers. Overwhelmed, he sweat on what to do. Suddenly, Lemma met him in a hologram beside him, pointing to a specific drawer. **"It's that one."**

Otis dashed to the indicated drawer, pulled it open, and retrieved a silver box. "What now?" he asked the hologram.

"You need to take it outside, press the button, and throw it."

"All that way? Five minutes will be gone before I know it."

"If that were the way out, you would never have survived as a race."

"So which is the way?"

"Run. I will lead you."

Otis nodded and began running, following the hologram. Meanwhile, Peter and Ernest watched on the mainframe as red solar radiation neared Earth. Their fingers peeled the leather off the seat in dire anxiety. "C'mon Otis! The World is counting on you boy!"

Otis raced through the edifice, the hologram guiding him until he reached a dead end. He stepped out into the glaring light of the sun. Taking a deep breath, he pressed the button on the box and tossed it into the air. The box transformed into a robot that soared out of view. The robot flew toward the power box, grasped it, and ascended beyond Earth's atmosphere just before the solar radiation struck. Otis watched in relief as the red sky gradually returned to normal, the temperature cooling. When the sky cleared completely, the power box dropped back to Earth, now covered in a silver sheen.

Otis fell back, unbelieving. His two hands had saved the World!

As he cried and joyed, Lemma's hologram hovered near him. **"You did well, KATO."**

Otis sat up, "Lemma, 8,000 years ago–how did you not help save Venus?"

"I was awakened at the very end. My maker limited my programming so

I could only respond to the escape instruction upon my full realisation. However, in my time here, I have watched how humans are. I suppose this and that civilization are not very different. Your politics and how your power structures have evolved—usually, a senseless fight of greed that culminates in wars. Perhaps that is what led to my Maker ridding Venus of a worse ending."

"The pods down there...Did everyone make it out alive?"

"I was programmed to harvest Venus's spawns every few years, depending on their survival integration to aid The Black race's earthers. The pods are all under my lifeline. They all made it."

"When was the last harvest?"

Lemma was quiet for a moment. **"21 earth years ago."**

"Wait, that's about the time I was...never mind. Do you have a record from that harvest?"

"I do. Are you looking for someone in particular?"

"Not quite—just out of curiosity."

"Very well. The last harvest was 3 individual spawns from the warrior faction."

Otis leaned in to see the 3. He was stuck on one of the three, puzzled. Then, the images glitched, and Lemma's hologram disappeared, leaving Otis with more questions than answers.

Otis emerged from the wall looking disgruntled and more confused. Ernest met him in cheer and pats on the back, "You did it, man!" Peter on the other hand paused, meeting Otis's line of sight giving a slight smile to his side. He mouthed, 'You saved us!'

A week later.

Otis stood beside a grave, sadness etched on his face as the man he had known as his father was laid to rest. Irene remained inside his arms weeping. He watched her shed all those bottled up tears. He felt the pain that was caged up in the shock and disillusion to survive, when she should have mourned. *'Closure, Finally.'*

Behind them, his friends watched solemnly–all in black attire.

After the body was interred, Otis took a handful of soil and poured it into the grave before stepping back. As he turned to leave, Ivy with a cast on her left arm, approached him, took his hand, and they walked away. "I still don't understand how he died that night," Otis said, his voice heavy with grief.

"The truth will come out in due time," Ivy replied.

At a distance, Ernest and Peter silently watched as Otis and Ivy walked away together.

Peter Wanjohi

Hailing from Nakuru, also the set locale for the events in the book, telling stories has been Peter's one ambition since High School.

Not just stories, but African stories!

He is the author of: *The Sasabonsam'*,

an African mythological novel about a West African vampire also going by the book's title.

'The Black' is his newest offering to every African Sci-fi and Fiction lover:

"Unveiling the past, one page at a time. Dive into a world where history and imagination intertwine- *The black*: a tale of secrets, power, and forgotten legacies."

-Peter Wanjohi, Author **'The Black'**

www.ingramcontent.com/pod-product-compliance
Lightning Source LLC
Chambersburg PA
CBHW010425120726
47992CB00008B/3326